NO SUNSHINE WITHOUT SHADOW

Anton Radinov had never known shadow in his life, for he was more fortunate than most, possessing good looks, wit, charm and something akin to genius in his acting career. But there was something he lacked — the ability to bring happiness into the life of his young and lovely wife, Ruth. Very soon, their lives were diverted on to separate paths. But true love never runs a straight course, and there's no sunshine without shadow.

PAULA LINDSAY

NO SUNSHINE WITHOUT SHADOW

Complete and Unabridged

LINFORD
Leicester

First published in Great Britain in 1957

First Linford Edition
published 2000

British Library CIP Data

Lindsay, Paula, *1933* –
    No sunshine without shadow.—Large print ed.—
    Linford romance library
    1. Love stories
    2. Large type books
    I. Title
    823.9'14 [F]

    ISBN 0–7089–5698–X

Published by
F. A. Thorpe (Publishing)
Anstey, Leicestershire

Set by Words & Graphics Ltd.
Anstey, Leicestershire
Printed and bound in Great Britain by
T. J. International Ltd., Padstow, Cornwall

This book is printed on acid-free paper

1

Anton stood in the wings of the Venus Theatre: in a few moments the curtain would rise on the last act of *A Question of Murder?*

He was a brilliant actor and acclaimed by critics all over the world. But he had worked for that acclaim; the long climb upwards had not been easy and he had been disappointed and disillusioned many times in his search for fame when he was a younger man. Now, at thirty-seven, he was at the top of his own particular tree.

Tall, handsome, endowed with a natural charm and a brilliant personality, Anton Radinov was the idol of hundreds who saw in him the symbol of their secret dreams. Many women were interested in Anton and they did not fail to let him know that he intrigued them. Anton, amused but indifferent, encouraged them all and flirted dangerously with a few. It was good publicity! It was no exaggeration that they spoke of him scornfully as a modern Don Juan.

But no woman ever regarded the danger signs — it was clear enough when Anton was tiring of an affair — and therefore he felt himself absolved from blame when their dreams crashed about their ears.

Hardly a week went by that Anton Radinov, son of a Russian father and an English actress mother, was not in the news — especially in the gossip columns — credited with another romance or admonished playfully because of one more escapade — some true, some false.

This present part in a gripping murder play by a well-known American authoress was one that Anton was particularly happy with. It gave him full scope for his dramatic ability. His leading lady, Avrina Marsh, was very lovely, a fine actress and one of the very few women who remained unmoved by Anton's charm. She made no secret of her contempt for his type of man!

The curtain rose and Anton strode on, assuming the necessary air of deep preoccupation and spoke his first lines as *Richard* to *Moyra*, played by Avrina Marsh.

The audience of several hundred tense and expectant theatre-goers who awaited his entrance emitted little sighs of relieved tension. His friends in their box at the side of the theatre tried in vain to catch his eye: he remained completely engrossed in his part. He had one peculiarity: he never encouraged any friends of his to visit him during the interval between acts; he preferred to be completely alone, able to relax and clear his mind completely in preparation for the act before him. But his friends were always welcome after the performance.

As usual, Anton's acting was superb, backed by Avrina's own brilliance: she had been a top-ranking actress for some years now. The play was tense. In this last act, Anton — as the bewildered, deeply anxious man just acquitted of the murder of his own child, having believed himself already on his way to the gallows through overpowering circumstantial evidence when he knew himself to be innocent — was magnificent.

Six months' familiarity with his part had not lessened the impact and Anton gave of his best at every performance. The critics were unanimously agreed that Anton Radinov was the actor of the year and this production his best play to date.

His friends were seeing the play for about the third time: all but Ruth Strong. Her cousin, David Harmer, was an up-and-coming young actor who clung to Anton's friendship in the hope that it would influence his future producers. He was a gay and unscrupulous young man whose charm and manners were carefully cultivated. He and Ruth were not particularly good friends, but he had been let down at the last minute by a girl-friend and he had suddenly thought of his cousin who was conveniently on the telephone. So he had rung her and offered her the pleasure of an evening in his company at the Venus Theatre, to see *A Question of Murder?* with Anton Radinov — and Ruth, who adored the theatre, had eagerly accepted.

She met David before the show: he was accompanied by a very *svelte* and elegant redhead, a stranger to Ruth, whose name was Rona Grant-Hawkeley, and a tall fair man by the name of Les Power, who was escorting Rona.

The play had captured Ruth's attention from the very beginning and she had been engrossed in it completely: but the stage was dead for her when Anton Radinov was not in the scene. She had never met him socially and she was looking forward to going behind-scenes with David, as he had already promised her. What a fine and handsome man Anton Radinov is, she mused, and a thrill shot through her at the thought of meeting him.

As the curtain fell, a sigh escaped Ruth. David looked at her and grinned: he was glad that she had come with them, after all. She was a pretty little thing and he had noticed Les giving her an appreciative glance occasionally. Of course, David thought, his eyes wandering to Rona, Ruth wasn't a patch on that lovely woman. Rona caught his glance and smiled slowly, seductively. It wasn't that David appealed to her so very much — how could he, when she adored Anton — but she could never resist turning her charm on any man. Lovely, *svelte*, amazingly elegant, Rona was the daughter of a baronet. She had spent all her adult life enjoying the arms and affections of man after man — but no man had ever affected her as strongly as Anton Radinov did now. Perhaps his fame and personable attraction had a lot to do with it, but she was head over heels in love with him. For some time now, he had been escorting her about town. They were quite frequently together and avid gossip-writers sought the scent of an engagement. Rona had never wanted marriage before: but this time she was eager to marry Anton and was fairly certain of her ability to do so, but she took great care not to count her chickens yet!

They made their way backstage to Anton's dressing-room, where he joined them as quickly as he could: they waited for him with a bottle of wine, already open and sampled. He was greeted warmly. Anton sank into a chair and smiled, a trifle wanly. Beneath his make-up he was pale and tired and needed rest, a few moments of solitude, but he could not tell his friends that. David poured him out a drink and handed it to him. Anton smiled his thanks.

'Did you all enjoy the show?' he asked, sipping his drink. Rona came over and dropped a light kiss on his forehead.

'A wonderful performance, darling,' she murmured. For a brief moment he caught her hand in his.

Ruth stood quietly and unassumingly, watching her cousin and his friends as they crowded round Anton. As yet, Anton had not even noticed her, but she didn't mind. It was enough to be able to study him unobtrusively. Suddenly David remembered her.

'Oh, Anton — you haven't met my cousin Ruth.' He turned to Ruth. 'Come and tell Anton how you loved the play — how you sat entranced the whole evening.' David drew her over to his friend, who took her hand, smiling.

'I didn't know David had such a charming cousin. So you liked the play?'

Ruth nodded, drawing her hand from his gently. She did not care for the general effusiveness of the theatrical world and he had held her hand a moment or two longer than was necessary.

Anton sat looking up at her: there was something about this very young and obviously shy girl that appealed to him strongly. She was a small girl, with a slender, trim figure: her black short evening dress contrasted with her honey-gold short curls which she pushed back from her forehead with a sudden, oddly graceful gesture, born of shyness as he studied her. There was a depth of serenity in her lovely grey eyes that stirred Anton unaccountably. He felt suddenly aware of her in the very depths of his being.

Perhaps Rona sensed this sudden attraction; in any case, she leaned over him to whisper in his ear. Her lovely breasts were deeply revealed by her low-cut evening gown and Anton's glance was unavoidably drawn to her beauty. Rona smiled intimately, confidently, and whispered something in his ear that Ruth did not catch. But she caught the tone of her voice:

soft and inviting, her eyes full of secret promise that was calculated to thrill even the most celibate of men. But Anton, raising his eyes to Ruth's, noticed that she had flushed, though very faintly, and suddenly he felt sickened by Rona's shamelessness. He looked from Ruth to Rona, meeting the latter's glowing green eyes. There was a sweet purity about Ruth's eyes that shamed the thoughts that Rona brought to mind. Anton brushed Rona aside, knocking the glass of wine from her hand accidentally. Anger made a bright flame of colour in her cheeks — anger at the rebuff more than the accident.

'Anton!' she exclaimed sharply. 'That was rather silly!'

David and Les, who had been talking together, were suddenly silent and they both noticed Rona's blazing eyes and her face, which was white with temper.

'I'm sorry, darling!' Anton said quickly. 'Les, give Rona another drink, will you. Then I must ask you all to clear out for a while — I must change.' He smiled at Rona to atone for his sharpness and reluctantly she returned the smile.

'We're throwing a party, Anton, old man,' David said quickly. 'So don't be too long, will you?'

Anton frowned. 'Do you really want me to come along? I don't feel in the mood for parties to-night.'

Rona laid her white, beautifully manicured hand on his shoulder. 'Darling, you'll enjoy it. You must come. Please?' For a moment he hesitated, then he nodded.

'Yes, all right. Give me fifteen minutes — and I'll be with you. Before, if I can manage it.' He turned to the mirror and began to remove his stage make-up with cream and tissues. Then he paused and watched them leave the room, a pensive look on his face. He was not very keen on the idea of yet another party. The original blank exhaustion he had felt had lifted, leaving only a partial tiredness, but a vague sense of depression haunted him. He wished that his friends could understand his need for peace and quiet. He was seldom in the mood for gay parties and merry crowds after a performance, but Rona and the others found that hard to understand. He took his time about changing, wishing that he did not have to rush off to his party to eat, drink and be merry — he would probably feel like death the next day, anyway!

The party was at Les's flat: he was a scenario artist and had many artist friends, several of whom turned up as the night wore on. Anton knew it would carry on into the very early hours of the morning, but he began to feel jaded before long.

He noticed that David's cousin seemed strangely out of place amongst this motley of people. David seemed to have forgotten her, and was steadily getting more and more drunk, flirting outrageously with a blonde model. Ruth sat by the window, quiet and unassuming. Occasionally, a man crossed over to speak to her, but although she answered and smiled at them, Anton noticed that, within a very few minutes, the man would make an excuse and wander off. He wondered idly where Rona was. She was usually at his elbow, but for once she neglected him. He looked round the room and saw her deep in conversation with Les, smiling up at him warmly, obviously expending her charm on him in a very generous manner. Absolved from the responsibility of looking after Rona, Anton wandered over to Ruth's side. She smiled up at him a trifle shyly.

'Lonely?' he asked, giving her a cigarette and then flicking his lighter for her. 'Would you like me to get you a drink? — your glass is empty.'

She shook her head. 'No, thanks. I'm not used to very much drink.'

'David isn't looking after you very well,' Anton said, glancing at David and frowning at his behaviour. Ruth followed his glance.

'Oh, I don't expect him to worry about me,' she told Anton quickly. 'It was nice of him to invite me out: we don't see very much of each other, really — and I certainly didn't expect to come on to a party.'

'I don't think you like parties, do you?' Anton divined shrewdly. She looked at him quickly, anxiously.

'Is it so obvious?' she asked. 'I'm trying to look as if I'm enjoying myself. I don't like this kind of party, I must admit.'

Anton grinned disarmingly. 'Would you like me to take you home?'

'Oh, no! I shall be all right,' she demurred, flushing slightly.

'I can assure you that David will be in no fit state to see you home by the time he is ready to leave!' Anton warned her, and took her arm. 'Come along. You'll be safer with me — even if you don't know me,' he teased. 'Where do you live?'

'South Kensington,' she told him.

'But please . . . don't bother. I can get a taxi home.'

'Nonsense! You're just the excuse I need to get away from this boring party.' He assured her of this with a smile, and she looked up at him quickly.

'Are you sure?' He nodded and she rose to her feet. They made their farewells, Anton merely nodding 'good night' to Rona who, suddenly aware that he was leaving, looked after him with anger in her eyes and hatred of Ruth by his side. How dare he take home that little chit? Or was it just a coincidence that they were leaving together? Knowing Anton, she doubted it very much. Why didn't David look after his cousin? Looking round for him, she soon discovered why! David was too engrossed in his blonde companion to have eyes for his cousin or anyone else.

Anton led Ruth to his old and rather shabby car. He was very fond of this car and remained loyal to her, although Rona had been trying for weeks to persuade him to buy a new and expensive model. He opened the door for Ruth and, when she was settled, strode round to his own side.

He was a careful and competent driver and Ruth enjoyed the journey through the deserted streets of London. It was a very wet night and Ruth leaned back in her seat, comfortable, secure and protected from the rain. It was a wonderful feeling. Anton glanced at her. She was looking a little tired and there was an air of youth and vulnerability about her as she relaxed, her guard down, and he felt a sudden tenderness towards her. She turned and looked at him. Meeting his eyes, she smiled shyly, thinking how the wan pallor of his face in the half-light accentuated his obvious tiredness — and thinking how penetrating yet impish his brilliant eyes were.

'Tired?' he asked gently, and she nodded.

'Yes. A little. It's so kind of you to

take me home, Mr. Radinov,' she said and he frowned.

'Call me Anton,' he told her. 'Don't let's be formal — you know, I can't understand why David has never mentioned you before.'

She laughed. 'I don't suppose he imagined that you'd be interested — why should you be?'

'David has little imagination, I'm afraid,' Anton said cuttingly, swerving round a corner so that Ruth was flung slightly against him. She straightened up. 'Sorry,' he said, smiling. That sudden warm smile went straight to her heart. Their eyes met briefly and Ruth knew that her heart leapt — an affinity was born in that brief moment. The wonder that was Anton fascinated her, held her spellbound. Since the first moment she had watched him walk on to the stage, earlier that evening, Ruth had experienced a strong magnetic draw towards this personable man. As Anton met her eyes, he felt a sudden beat-missing bound of his heart and the blood pounded in his ears. He felt a spiritual contact as he gazed deeply into her serene grey eyes. Driven by impulse, Anton took his hand from the driving-wheel and laid it on hers for a brief, intimate moment, smiling down at her. Then, with an obvious effort, brought his mind back to the road.

At least, part of his mind. He could not help thinking idly how pretty her honey-coloured hair was, how sweetly it curled around her well-shaped small head. How grey and candidly lovely her eyes were: he remembered their sweet expression, frank, open and unashamed. Her eyes were very expressive and Anton felt sure that she found it hard to hide her thoughts and emotions with eyes like she possessed.

Ruth felt as though not only had he reached out to touch her with his hand, but also as though she had experienced a spiritual contact that made her whole body tremble. Neither could have explained satisfactorily the sense of intimacy that surrounded them. No words were spoken or needed — yet they communed with each other in silence.

Anton drove quickly and before long they reached South Kensington. Here, Ruth broke the silence to give Anton directions. She had a tiny flat in a large Georgian house. She lived alone, quite happily, amongst her own possessions. Ruth enjoyed leading her own life and being quite independent and free to do as she pleased. She worked for an advertising agency and her salary was supplemented by a small income from her father, which enabled her to live comfortably. Her family home was in Sussex, but she very rarely went home, now that she lived in London.

When they arrived at Ruth's address, they stood by the car for a few moments, chatting idly. Ruth thanked him again for his kindness. Before she went in, he took her hand and, leaning forward, kissed her briefly on the forehead.

'Good night, Ruth. Sleep well!' Then he watched her as she ran up the steps and let herself in.

As she prepared for bed, rather slowly, due to her thoughts of Anton, she let her dreams have full rein. Always a dreamer possessed of a vivid imagination, she wove colourful fantasies about Anton. But she knew in her heart that Anton would probably never give her another thought — he surely kissed every woman he took home from a party — and no doubt far more warmly, which surely should teach her not to weave such romantic dreams when all she had received was a light, cool kiss on her brow.

Lying between soft, cool linen, Ruth knew that she had fallen in love. She always had believed in love at first sight, but never experienced it. Yet she had instantly recognized the emotion. From the moment she had set eyes on Anton, when he walked on to the stage at the beginning of the evening, her heart had been lost to him, and irrevocably. She wondered what it would be like if Anton were to love her in return, perhaps even want to marry her — but even while she wondered, she fell asleep.

Anton, meanwhile, drove home to his mews flat. He whistled blithely as he ran up the stairs and opened the door with his key. Then the tune died as he saw Rona's beautiful white fur stole (which had cost him quite a lot of money) flung across a chair just inside the door. He strode to the lounge and went in. Rona was sitting on the divan, smoking her own special brand of French cigarettes in a long jet cigarette-holder. A glass half-full of wine stood on the low table in front of her.

'Hallo, darling!' she greeted him, holding out her hand to him. 'I was bored at the party, so I thought I'd come along here for some entertainment. But you weren't here for your poor little Rona to come home to — so I waited.'

'So I see!' He flung his coat, scarf and gloves on to a chair and helped himself to a drink, ignoring her outstretched hand. 'There are times when I wish I hadn't given you a key to this flat.'

'Darling! Are you angry with me?' She rose and went over to him, putting an arm about his neck. 'You weren't involved with a pretty little popsy — as I half suspected — so it didn't matter, did it?'

'The popsy being David's cousin?' Anton queried dryly. Rona laughed.

'Perhaps! Aren't you glad I came, darling?' She kissed his throat where the pulse beat a little unsteadily. He slid his arms around her, his senses stirred as always by her nearness. Their lips met. Rona clung to him with sudden passion.

'Love me?' he asked, gently nuzzling her throat. She smiled triumphantly over his shoulder.

'Of course. You know you're irresistible,' she teased him.

'I thought you found Les Power

more attractive this evening,' he said casually.

'Darling!' she exulted. 'Don't tell me you were jealous? Les and I were discussing the scenery he's going to design for my Christmas show — you know I always organize a charity 'do' at home.' She caressed the nape of his neck, teasingly, and raised her mouth to be kissed.

'You can't blame me for wondering why you were so interested in him,' Anton said, then kissed her.

She returned his kiss with a burning passion.

'You're wonderful,' he murmured, straining her to him. She relaxed, deliberately provocative, and for a few moments longer she stood in the circle of his arms, seeking his lips.

He released her and said casually, 'Well, now that you're here, you might as well stay.'

With a brief sigh of relief, Rona knew that once again she had triumphed.

2

It was late when Ruth awoke the next morning, so late that the rather watery sun, high in the sky, finally penetrated her restless dreams. She rolled over sleepily, then sat up to glance at her watch. It was twenty to eleven, which was very late for Ruth, who was usually an early riser. She sat up in bed, glad that, as it was a Saturday morning, she wasn't due at the advertising agency.

She remembered that she had been later to bed than was usual the night before. A slow smile curved her lips as she remembered even more. Sinking back into the warm softness of her blankets, she relived the previous evening: the exciting intensity of the play, the unusual attentions of her cousin David, meeting the star, Anton Radinov, backstage when the performance was over, and then the party. Was it really true that Anton Radinov, sensing her loneliness, had gone out of his way to be friendly to her, had even brought her home in his car? Had he really leaned forward to kiss her forehead? Childlike, she touched her temple as if to find some remaining sign of the caress.

Ruth, sighing, knew that she had been a different person when she left Anton. He had had some strange effect on her. He was undoubtedly a charming and very attractive man — yet she was sure that he hadn't set out to impress her with his charm. Ruth felt that he was sincere and unaffected.

She was a warm-hearted girl, but she was not easily swayed by men's attentions. Although she had never experienced the real impact of a deep and lasting affection for any man, she was full of an emotion this morning which she felt sure could only be defined as love. As she lay thinking of Anton, she knew that he was the only man who would matter in her life, and that she was already irrevocably bound to him by some strange affinity that she only vaguely sensed and could not determine. She smiled to herself. It was foolish, she knew, to fall in love with a man over the footlights of a theatre — and especially with a man like Anton Radinov, whose reputation with women was well known. She frowned: was it really true that he was a rake? She could not reconcile it with her impression of him.

Ruth flung back her covers, convinced that in the future her life was going to be affected by Anton to a very great extent. Foolish or otherwise, she loved him! She longed to fly into his arms and hold him close, telling him of her love. It would be wonderful beyond her dreams to have him fall in love with her.

She stood by the window for a few minutes, indulging in wonderful day-dreams in which she attained her heart's desire — and was the envy of all women because she had married Anton

Radinov! Fanciful weavings of a vivid imagination. She knew, in her heart, that they could not possibly come true. And — she finally admonished herself — even if they did, it was no insurance for happiness. Or Anton's happiness, which was far more important.

All her life she had been waiting for a man like Anton to transform her very being — now that she had met the one man who would ever mean anything to her, there wasn't very much likelihood that her love would be of any avail. She felt suddenly depressed. If Anton was still a bachelor after all these years, it didn't seem as though the prospect of marriage appealed to him very much — what hope had Ruth of changing his mind?

* * *

Anton rose late, as was his custom, then dressed and shaved leisurely.

He lunched with Flavek, his manager, a business lunch that was merely an

27

excuse for discussion regarding a new play, but nevertheless he enjoyed the meal. Afterwards, he drove Flavek to his office, then went on to the theatre, where he called in for a brief chat with the producer. Then he drove to Rona's flat. He wondered how she would receive him after his abrupt refusal of her favours the night before.

Anton wondered idly, as he drove, what had made him change his mind — holding Rona in his arms, swept by the tide of passion — yet he had felt a strange aloofness, seemed to stand away and look at the spectacle of himself clinging to a shallow, eager woman. He had felt disgust and sudden contempt for the power she possessed over his senses and, releasing her without warning, Anton had hurried her from the flat. Rona had been startled and angry, but she had gone, flouncing away in a temper, refusing his offer to drive her home.

When Anton arrived, late though it was, Rona was still wandering around in a housecoat, smoking. The radiogram was switched on and a plaintive melody drifted through the flat. She turned, surprised, as Anton was ushered in by her maid and two bright spots of angry colour flamed in her cheeks.

'Why, hallo! I didn't expect to see *you!*'

'Were you expecting someone else?' Anton countered, smiling at her. He threw his gloves down on the table and looked at her with admiration in his eyes. She was undoubtedly a lovely woman. The colour in her cheeks enhanced the brilliance of her unusual green eyes; her hair was a rare shade of pure auburn and kept long in defiance of fashion. Now her hair nestled gently on her milky white shoulders, which were revealed by the low-cut housecoat as it slipped gently from her throat and shoulders, to fall in a cascade of shimmering green satin — almost the exact shade of her eyes. All her clothes were beautiful and well chosen.

Her eyes narrowed. 'Not exactly. But

I thought you were the last person to come knocking on my door to-day.'

'Why?' He offered her a cigarette and she selected one carefully, tapped it on her thumbnail and waited for him to produce a light before she answered, with a provocative flash from those exciting eyes: 'You weren't exactly glad of my company last night, were you?'

He looked deeply into her eyes for a brief moment, standing tall and masculine and very close to her. She felt her anger against him slowly fading. 'I'm afraid I was rather foolish last night, my sweet. My only plea is that it was very late and I was tired.'

'Poor Anton!' she sympathized, her voice calculatingly low and seductive. 'You always seem so tired lately — ' She paused, then went on, smiling at him with a question in her eyes: 'Is it because you're working too hard or are you simply tiring of me?'

'Being a woman, you *would* think that. It seems to be the first thing that leaps to a woman's mind, but it isn't

30

true, in this case.' He turned away and walked over to the window: he stood there for a few moments, gazing idly down at the traffic below. 'You're not the type of woman a man tires of easily, my dear. You weave an exciting web that keeps me firmly ensnared.' He turned back into the room and held her eyes boldly.

'At least you don't sound regretful,' she said, smiling provocatively. He strode across and pulled her into his arms, kissing her savagely. For a brief moment she resisted him, angry that he could treat her so — she was a fool to be so much in love with him that she was powerless to resist his charm — and his kisses . . . She melted against him.

He suggested a drive and she nodded, assenting eagerly. She went into her bedroom to change; she was gay and laughing, excited at the prospect of going out. Rona felt stifled when she was indoors — especially when she was alone. Anton waited, lounging against the window, smoking. Occasionally, they exchanged a few words. Suddenly, he stiffened, as he caught sight of a familiar figure in the street below. Surely he recognized that golden head held high and the trim figure beneath it. He watched Ruth walk down the busy street.

'What are you watching so intently, Anton?' Rona came and stood beside him, smoothing her gloves over her wrists.

'Nothing,' Anton replied. 'I thought I saw someone I knew, but I was mistaken.' He turned away and stood watching her. She had changed into a lime green suit with tan accessories and looked very smart and attractive. She would be an asset to any man as his wife — he wondered if he would ever marry her. He knew that she would willingly agree to the suggestion — without conceit, Anton knew that Rona was madly in love with him. They were good friends, two of a type, and they understood each other — or was it merely superficial understanding,

Anton wondered, for he never felt any real affinity with Rona, merely a strong stirring of the senses. She was not a restful woman. Her attraction, physical and magnetic, never let him be: strong though that attraction might be now — in a few years time the flame would probably turn to ashes. It was inevitable that such physical fascination should die, leaving nothing worthwhile in its wake. The thought of Ruth came to his mind. He realized wryly that he was not even aware of her surname. There was something different about her, an unusual air of serenity, of peace. He remembered her candid grey eyes, the sweet expression of her mouth with its joyful love-of-living lift and the proud yet unassuming way in which she held that golden head. Anton felt that behind her apparent shyness there was hidden depths of a rich, warm and glowing nature. He remembered too the feeling of spiritual contact in the half-lit intimacy of the car, on the night of their first meeting — and the sudden impulse which had impelled him to touch her hand with his. Had he imagined the warm response in her lovely eyes? He wondered idly, fleetingly, if there were any men in her life. If she cared for some man and hoped to marry him?

Anton suddenly felt that he would like to marry Ruth. With her for his wife he could be sure of peace, harmony and constant affection, a pleasant home that really was home. His flat was luxurious and very comfortable, but something was missing. Ruth would never be demanding or possessive or wilful — and surely when he was in the grip of one of his savage black moods which seemed to be getting more and more frequent, then Ruth would understand and help him, respecting his need of silent comfort.

He dismissed the subject as Rona took his arm and they left her flat together. It was an interesting idea and he would go over it in his mind another time.

Rona, unaware of the reason for his thoughtfulness, was annoyed at his strange silence, but she laughed up at him as they made their way down to his car. 'Dreamer! Wake up and tell me where we are going?'

'Mm? Oh, yes. Well, wherever you like, my dear.' He smiled down at her and suddenly he laid his hand on hers and pressed it. 'You're a lovely woman, Rona!' he murmured. She laughed and got into the car.

'Darling! How sweet of you to say so,' she replied in her low musical voice.

'Not sweet at all!' he retorted, swinging himself into the driving-seat and turning the ignition key. 'Just truthful.' He released the brake and they shot off down the road in search of adventure.

★ ★ ★

Gregg Randall glanced at his watch. It was unlike Anton to be late, but it was already ten minutes past the hour they had arranged to meet. Gregg was one of Anton's greatest friends. They had been together in a production called *Laughing Criminal* four years earlier and had recognized in each other a kindred spirit. Since then they had retained a warm regard for each other. Even as he looked up from his wrist, Anton entered the restaurant. Tall, handsome in an immaculate grey suit, he walked with a distinguished air that commanded attention from those around him. He approached Gregg, smiling.

'Sorry I'm so late. I tried to be here on time, but I was discussing plans with Flavek and Sol Kester for a new play and we got rather involved . . . '

'That's all right, old man. Sit down.' Gregg had risen to shake hands with him. As soon as they were both seated, a waiter hurried up to them. Gregg ordered the meal competently and decisively. Then he turned to Anton as the waiter left them. 'So you really mean to leave the Venus productions?'

'It's a possibility. I'm beginning to feel a little stale. And this new play is really rather brilliant' — Anton leaned forward, his eyes shining with sudden enthusiasm — 'just my meat!'

'Probably everyone else's poison!' Gregg commented dryly, his eyes twinkling. 'I only hope *A Question of Murder?* doesn't go down the drain without you, Anton!'

'I've recommended Kim Sinclair as my replacement. I don't know if he's worth such a recommendation, but there's no harm in giving him a trial. I like the way he handles *Steven* at the moment.'

'With your reference he's a made man. But, of course, you know that!' Gregg produced cigarettes and offered them to Anton, who shook his head. 'Perhaps you don't agree that you have much influence, though?' Gregg went on, raising an eyebrow in query.

'Oh, I don't know.' Anton answered

slowly, thoughtfully. 'I don't care to recommend people as a rule — they so often let one down — but old Sol Kester seemed lost for a new lead and I suddenly thought of Sinclair. He really *is* good' — again that sudden burst of enthusiasm — 'and if he reaches the top it will be on his own merits, not my recommendation!' There was a pause in the conversation while they were deftly served by deferential waiters. Very little was said during the meal, which was perfectly prepared and served. As they sat over coffee and cigarettes, Anton was silent, wondering whether or not to tell Gregg about his plans for marrying Ruth. He had finally — after much thought — decided that it would be to his advantage to make her his wife. She was quite delightful. He had taken her to lunch during the week and found her to be good company, peaceful and intelligent, quite well read. She was sweet and charming, and when he was with her he had felt again that odd stirring in his heart. He knew that he would never marry Rona — or her type of woman — and that if he was ever married at all it would be to a girl like Ruth. Now that he was nearing forty he began to feel the need of marriage to a restful woman, who would add even more to the comfort of his home life.

Anton felt at ease and perfectly relaxed, as he always did with Gregg, who was reliable and sincere, and yet a man of the world who understood Anton as no man had ever done. He would never condemn him for his morals or general behaviour. Gregg believed that tolerance was the only important virtue and did his best to live by this maxim.

Anton suddenly stubbed his cigarette in the ash-tray in front of him and straightened in his seat.

'I'm thinking of getting married, Gregg!' he said quietly. Gregg stared at him, then grinned.

'Are you serious? You've said that before — but nothing has ever come of it.'

'Quite serious this time. No joking, Gregg.'

'Congratulations are in order in that case. I wondered if Rona would ever get you as far as the church door,' Gregg commented idly.

'It isn't Rona!' Anton smiled as he delivered his bombshell. He knew that Gregg would be surprised.

'Not Rona?' Gregg exclaimed. 'Good lord! That's a sock in the eye for the gossip-writers!' Anton laughed. 'Everyone's expecting it to be Rona,' Gregg continued. 'Are you pulling my leg?'

'I know it's the expected thing. That's why — *not* Rona!' Anton leaned forward. 'Of course, you must keep this to yourself. When I do marry, it will be secretly. I can't afford to lose my eligibility in the gossip-writers' eyes. No one must even have the scent of the news.'

Gregg grinned. 'I presume you'll tell the recipient of your affections — who is she, anyway?'

'You've probably never heard of her. Her name is Ruth. Cousin to David Harmer. A very sweet and attractive girl.'

'Obviously *you* think so — otherwise you wouldn't be thinking of her as a possible wife. What is it, Anton — the urge to settle down?' He grinned.

Anton nodded. 'Something like that. I feel that it's time I was married and she's the only one I could stand for the rest of my life, day in, day out.'

'Lucky girl! What's got into you, Anton? I shouldn't have thought you the marrying type under any circumstances!' Anton laughed at Gregg's remark.

'I know,' he confirmed, 'but a man can change his mind. After all, Gregg, I'm thirty-seven — I begin to feel that a home with a young and adoring wife might be rather an attractive proposition.'

'Someone to go home to?' Gregg nodded understandingly. He paused, then added warningly: 'Rona will be furious. You've rather led her up the garden path, Anton.'

'Nonsense! I've never suggested marriage to her,' Anton protested. 'But there's no reason why she should learn about Ruth. Rona's a damn attractive woman.' He paused. 'Why shouldn't I carry on . . . escorting her socially?' He deliberately broke his sentence with an impish light in his eyes. Gregg frowned, taking out his case. Both men took cigarettes and Gregg lighted both before replying.

He inhaled deeply and then said: 'Your wife — if you do marry — if you're serious about this — isn't going to approve. Unless she's extremely sophisticated and wants to lead an independent life, she'll want the whole world to know what a wonderful man she's married.' He grinned. 'Question-mark in brackets, needless to say! Anyway, she'll want to gloat over the other hopefuls she's beaten to the post. Providing she's a normal woman, that is.'

'I shall naturally explain matters to Ruth and I'm sure she'll agree to my suggestion of secrecy.' Anton drew on his cigarette. 'It must be obvious, Gregg, that I'm not in love with Ruth. I simply want a wife who will keep my house in order, as it were, someone with whom I can relax. Someone who isn't demanding of my time, because I won't have much to give her. She'll have to learn to be there when I want her and the first thing she'll learn is not to intrude when I don't.'

'Rather a tall order!' his friend commented acidly. He was not at all happy about Anton's ideas. Surely he'd never find any woman to submit to such a marriage. Anton had been born a little too late for such drastic and mid-Victorian expectations of his wife's attitude towards marriage.

'Nevertheless, I feel sure that Ruth will consent,' Anton said complacently.

'Why should she? Is she in love with you?'

'Possibly. Not as far as I know,

though. We only met a fortnight ago,' Anton told him.

'You appear to have made your mind up very quickly,' Gregg said a little scathingly. 'I have a strong feeling that you will receive an unpleasant rebuff from this Ruth of yours when you put forward such a one-sided argument for wedding-bells. Unless, of course, she's a most unusual woman — tell me, Anton, what does she get out of marrying you?'

'Something that most women would give their ears for — Anton Radinov as a husband!' Anton grinned. 'That sounds conceited, I know, but when one reads and hears such romantic piffle for long enough, I wonder if there isn't a grain of truth to be found in all the fables.' He smoothed back his dark, glossy hair with a casual gesture and brushed a speck of cigarette ash from his lapel. 'She'll have plenty of money — beautiful clothes, a lovely home; I'm thinking of buying a country cottage, Gregg, once we're married. A girl like

Ruth will be quite contented with such things.'

'And not even the satisfaction of having the world know that she's your wife?' Gregg was ironic. 'I'm sure there are plenty of women who would be contented with such an arrangement — no doubt there is a certain type of woman who would jump at it — but I sincerely hope for the poor girl's sake that this Ruth has far more spirit than to accept your amazingly generous offer!'

'You're being very satirical, old man. Let me tell you, Gregg, that I firmly believe Ruth *will* marry me. Without hesitation!' Anton told him decidedly.

'Then she's a fool!' Gregg said heatedly. His temper was roused; not surprising when one took into account his dark auburn head and the Irish blue of his eyes.

'I can't see that she's getting such a bad bargain . . . ' Anton protested.

'Although you mean to be such a wonderful husband that Rona will still be your constant companion?' Gregg interrupted him angrily, his eyes flashing. 'Far be it from me to condemn you, my friend, but I personally think that you're making a mistake! I haven't met this prospective wife of yours, but I feel in my bones that she isn't the type to appreciate your ideas on marriage!'

Anton shrugged and rose to his feet. 'Well, I'm sorry if you feel like that, but I'm sure you'll be proved wrong. I must be on my way. Can I give you a lift anywhere?'

Nodding, Gregg rose too, having settled the bill, and they left the restaurant together.

3

Anton paused with his hand on the
receiver. Should he ring Ruth and
suggest lunch? For he wanted to see
her, to be with her. She was restful and
this morning he was in need of rest.

Having made up his mind to his own
satisfaction that he would make Ruth
his wife one day in the not-too-distant
future, Anton had put her to the back
of his mind and concentrated on having
a good time with Rona and their mutual
friends for the time being. But this
morning he had woken with a vague
resentment against Rona, the recent
gay fling and the world in general.
What did it gain him — the constant
hunt for excitement and novelty? Late
nights only meant that he woke the
next day feeling disgruntled and weary.
And surely such hectic nights could not
continue much longer without affecting

47

his work: he knew that already his acting was beginning to suffer slightly — fortunately only enough for him to notice and not the critics. He could imagine the comments if they did: *'Losing your grip, old man?' 'Woman trouble, Anton?' 'What's the matter, Radinov? Too many revivers in the intervals, eh?'* Just as well that plans were going ahead for a new play in the autumn; he was definitely growing stale in his part. Already *Richard* wasn't so real to him: when he spoke his lines they were gradually becoming just lines and not tense reality as he had always before thought of them. Anton did not know whether it was the thought of Ruth or the actuality of Rona that played such havoc with his concentration. But whatever it was, he knew that he needed Ruth to-day — needed her with an intensity that he had never experienced in his physical need of Rona. There were times when he was gripped with a spiritual loneliness and dread, the strength of which made him

48

bitter and morose. He knew that this was one of those times — he had woken with the familiar feeling of depression. He felt that Ruth had the power to ease the lonely dread and so now he was in need of her. He felt angry with himself for neglecting her. Though it was a month since their first meeting, he had seen very little of her. He had phoned her on a few occasions, had taken her to lunch twice and he had met her at a cocktail party given by Jay Scott, the critic, only the week before. Apart from this, they had had no contact.

'That's no way to persuade a girl that you're the man she should marry,' he said aloud, reproaching himself. 'If I know anything of women, they prefer to be swept off their feet!'

He recalled the conversation he had had with Ruth's cousin, David Harmer, at the same cocktail party. Jay had been hovering around Ruth at the time and David had commented on it.

'She's very appealing,' Anton had

replied in answer to David's remark. 'It isn't surprising that even Jay is attracted to her.'

'But he's such a woman hater!' David had exclaimed.

'Not to that extent. He mentioned Ruth in his column after she went to the theatre with you, you know.'

'Did he?' David was startled. 'I didn't read it.'

'Oh, he merely remarked in that satirical way he has that Rona attended the Venus accompanied by two men (he gave both your names, by the way — most generous of him) and a stranger to town, a lovely who was set fair to putting Rona's nose out of joint!'

David had grinned his appreciation. 'I bet Rona was delighted by his frankness!'

'She was furious. She hasn't entirely forgiven him yet.' Anton smiled. 'Actually, pretty though Ruth may be, she isn't my type,' he added idly, as Jay came over to join them.

One had to be careful of one's words in the critic's company, he was apt to put his own interpretation on even the lightest remark.

'Just as well, perhaps, for the poor girl's sake,' Jay had chimed in, over-hearing his last words.

'Don't disillusion David!' Anton had said quickly. 'He thinks I'm as pure as the driven snow. You know, thinks there's no one like me, Jay!'

'I may think you're a pretty wonderful actor,' David had laughed, 'but no one — not even your best friends — could say that your private life is beyond reproach!'

'Like Cæsar's wife?' Anton had replied, and there had been a chorus of laughter. The conversation then turned to more general subjects.

Ruth had been deep in conversation with two young men who were artist friends of Les Power. If she had noticed Anton's arrival, she made no sign of it and he bided his time before going over to greet her. Then she smiled up at him warmly. Anton, looking down at her with new eyes, thinking of her as a prospective wife, was pleased with what he saw.

Having thought it over, Anton lifted the receiver and dialled Ruth's office number. He listened to the ringing tone, whistling softly under his breath, but before Gresham's had a chance to answer, a ring at his front door disturbed Anton and he replaced the telephone.

He went to answer the door rather reluctantly, for he did not feel in the mood for visitors. Opening the door, he was surprised to find Ruth standing there.

'Why, hallo, Ruth!' he said warmly.

'Hallo, Anton. Are you busy — am I disturbing you?' She spoke diffidently: the hot colour rose and stained her cheeks.

'Of course I'm not busy. Come in, my dear. I'm only too glad to see you.' He drew her in, closing the door. He saw nothing strange in her arrival on his doorstep, and it didn't occur to him that it might have cost Ruth any effort or that she might be regretting her sudden impulse to call on him. It had taken her several hours of indecision and much thought to finally convince herself that there was nothing extraordinary about the visit. She had been very miserable during the past week, so helplessly in love with Anton, longing to see him and despairing that her love could ever mean anything to him, certain that he would brush it aside in the same way that he shook off other women's love. His affairs were common knowledge, especially the heartless way in which he rid himself of women who became simply an annoyance. But she longed so much to see him that she had discarded all pride and set out for his flat. Now that she was here her courage deserted her — she was tongue-tied and flushed and angry with herself for it. 'Slip your coat off, Ruth. I'll make you some coffee.' He helped her off with her coat.

'Please don't bother with coffee,' she protested, 'thank you very much.' He smiled at her. She was very sweet and so unassuming. Rather lovely to-day, too, with the pinkness of her cheeks making her eyes bright and sparkling. He didn't know it was trepidation that made her lower lip tremble gently as he looked at her, but it was very appealing.

'Nonsense! I was just going to have some myself,' he assured her, 'but I hate drinking alone — even coffee — so you've come at the right time.' He went into the tiny kitchen and attended to the percolator. When he returned to the lounge, Ruth was standing by the window. She wore an emerald green dress which clung to her slim figure and made her look very slight. Anton, glancing at her as he bent to pick up a cigarette-box from the low table in the centre of the room, thought that she had an ethereal — almost untouchable — look about her, an air of fragility and vulnerability. He offered her a cigarette, crossing to her side, but did not take one himself.

'Aren't you smoking?' she asked, raising her head from the light he offered to gaze up at him in query. They were very close and Anton did not answer for a moment, trying to repress the sudden desire to touch her soft lips with his own. He looked into her eyes, then smiled.

'No. Not just now. I'm trying to cut down on smoking, the vice is getting too strong a hold lately.' Ruth nodded. 'By the way, aren't you at the office to-day?' Anton asked her. 'Come into money?'

She smiled. 'No. I wish I had — although I enjoy work. I decided to take a week's holiday — an early one, I know, but I'm going home to Sussex to-morrow. My father has been ill and he wants to see me.'

'Whereabouts in Sussex is your home, Ruth?'

'Latimer,' she replied. 'It's near Arundel.'

'Oh, yes, I know Latimer. I like Sussex. It's a very lovely county.'

She nodded, looking about the room, which was long and low-ceilinged, beautifully furnished. Almost too luxurious for a mere male who lived alone, she thought idly. She crossed to his bookcases which ran the length of one wall. He watched her. 'You like books?' he asked.

She threw him a quick glance over her shoulder. 'Very much. I'm an inveterate reader.'

'I guessed so. I must be cultivating insight.'

She turned and looked at him deliberately. 'I should have thought you already possessed that. Can one give so much to acting without insight? Surely you have to get right under the skin of a character from the very beginning — you have to understand and appreciate him fully. Doesn't that require insight?'

'Yes, I suppose it does. You know, Ruth, that's how *I* feel — about

56

getting right under the skin of a character, I mean,' Anton said in sudden enthusiasm. 'Exactly how I feel. I know *Richard* intimately now — but I had to study him. Now I know when a line of his is out of character — and it annoys me intensely when I have to say something in the guise of *Richard* that I damn well *know* he wouldn't say, normally, if he were reality and not fantasy!'

'There can't be many lines like that in such a wonderful play,' Ruth protested. 'She wouldn't be such a good playwright if any of her 'people' were out of character at all.'

Anton shrugged. 'Well, to others, perhaps the lines aren't out of character — but I know *Richard*! . . . ' He broke off, and grinned ruefully. 'Sorry. I'm getting rather carried away.'

'I understand,' Ruth told him gently. All trace of discomfort at calling on him in this unconventional way had gone. She was now perfectly at ease.

'Yes.' He paused, studying her. 'Yes,

you do understand,' he said slowly. 'I feel you always would — not many people do, you know!'

'Why not? It must be obvious . . . '

'Oh, they usually think my work is going to my head,' Anton laughed. 'They may be right at that — who knows?' With that, he remembered the percolator. 'Oh, Lord! The coffee! I won't be a minute.' So saying, he tore out to the kitchen.

Ruth looked after him, a tender look in her eyes. He could be very boyish — in his enthusiasm he had relaxed completely, gazing down at her with shining eyes. She turned back to his books after a moment and drew one out with interest. She was skimming through it, completely engrossed, so did not hear his returning step on the thick carpet. She was startled when he spoke.

'Good heavens, did I make you jump? I'm sorry.'

'I was interested in this.' She indicated her book. He glanced over her shoulder

58

at the book and nodded.

'Yes, that's a brilliant piece of writing. You've never read it?' He crossed the room to place the tray he carried on the low table. She shook her head in answer to his query. 'Well, put it down now and come and have some coffee,' he told her lightly. She obeyed and went to sit by him on the settee.

'I'm afraid you'll have to keep me well away from books of any kind if you want intelligent conversation out of me,' she told him, smiling, as she took the cup from his hand. 'I'm liable to forsake the world of reality for the realms of fiction at the slightest opportunity.'

Anton smiled, deciding that she had a pleasing voice; moderate, rather lilting with a very faint suggestion of huskiness. She chose her words well, too.

'I think you must be a dreamer, Ruth,' Anton said idly, sipping his coffee reflectively. 'A spectator in life rather than a runner,' he added.

'Running is so exhausting,' she smiled. 'I'm lazy. Besides, one never seems to catch up. I'd rather leave the usual frantic chase after excitement to others. I'm quite happy to watch them hunt than to join in the sport.'

'Silly child,' Anton admonished playfully, although inwardly he knew he agreed with her. 'You're missing a lot.' He paused to replace his cup on the tray, then went on: 'But who's to say you aren't the wisest. So far, you've sought nothing, discovered nothing, have all your illusions left, I imagine — and, what is most important, have your life before you to enjoy, new experiences to welcome . . .'

Not liking his rueful tone, Ruth interrupted eagerly: 'So have you, Anton.'

Ignoring her, he went on: 'You sit back and wait for life to come to you, instead of going out to find it too soon. I think perhaps you are a very *lucky* child. Not so silly, after all. Perhaps you're living your life in a more sensible way than I am.'

'Lucky, perhaps,' Ruth replied, 'Child, no! I'm twenty-three.' She said it with a mature air that made Anton smile.

'I repeat — child! To me, you're still an infant. If not in years, then in worldly knowledge. D'you know how old I am?'

Ruth laughed. 'Does anyone? Or have you been so very careful to keep it a secret?'

'Heavens, no! I'm not a Hollywood film star striving for eternal youth, you know. I'm thirty-seven, past the first flush of youth and willing to tell the world!' he exclaimed.

'Thirty-seven isn't old for a man,' Ruth declared. Anton gave a sudden peal of laughter. She was indeed very sweet.

'And for a woman?' he queried, with an air of great amusement.

'Women are different,' Ruth told him, quite seriously. 'They mature so much earlier than men.'

'My sweet Ruth! How wonderful

to have your youthful outlook!' Ruth flushed at the patronizing tone. 'What I envy most is your self-possession!' Anton went on. 'Youth is so complacently sure of it's acceptance in the world.'

'Is that wrong?' Ruth asked quietly.

'No, not wrong.' Anton sobered, remembering his own heady youth. 'Merely rather shattering. The world is not kind to newcomers — the already established inmates resent 'new boys' and at first pretend they don't exist, but eventually they are forced to accept them on sufferance — after that, it isn't very long before the erstwhile newcomer is being just as resentful and cruel towards an even newer 'boy'.'

'How cynical you are!' Ruth said, looking at him with new interest. She had not been allowed such an insight to his thoughts before. She studied the arrogant lift of the well-modelled head, the almost perfect cut of the features, the sensitive, temperamental mouth which was his weakest yet strongest feature: the piercing blue eyes which could blaze or smoulder and turn any woman's resistance to ashes if he chose. His hands were long, slender, with tapering fingers, well-manicured, expressive and strong: hands were one of the first things Ruth noted in a man and she approved Anton's once again.

'I'm thirty-seven,' Anton repeated, reminding her. 'One doesn't get to my age without acquiring a certain veneer of cynicism. Most of my illusions were shattered long before I was your age.'

'It must have been horrible for you, Anton,' she said swiftly, impulsively, prompted by a deep and sudden pity for the boy he must have been once — sensitive, immature, defenceless against the cruelty of the world.

'Why do you say that?' Anton was taken aback. Ruth seemed to sense bitterness behind his words that had not been apparent in his voice. Was this young girl capable of even deeper insight than she had already shown? He had been hurt and disillusioned in his youth — but he had believed that everyone had to grow up in such a way, be disillusioned so quickly and bitterly, but surely it was not so, he thought now, looking at Ruth in wonder at her air of general innocence and candour. He felt a surge of strong protective feeling and he hoped that Ruth would never be hurt, never know bitterness. He said now: 'That was an unusual thing to say!'

'Yes. But I believe it was applicable,' she replied, smiling gently at him.

'It was, but how could you know?'

'Insight?' she teased, leaning forward to stub out her cigarette, suddenly shy as their eyes met. A silence fell between them: not the uncomfortable silence experienced by two people who are comparative strangers, but the sudden intimate hush of affinity. Anton leaned back, smoking, having lit a cigarette some few moments earlier. After a while, he glanced at her.

'Bored?' he asked.

'Not at all. Should I be?' she countered. He shrugged.

'Most women expect me to entertain them — or make love to them; it usually amounts to the same thing. It's a change to find someone different, who doesn't expect that.'

'As for entertainment, well, you're not a performing seal,' Ruth protested. 'I don't expect you to balance a ball on your nose or perform party tricks . . .' her voice trailed off, as she met his amused eyes.

'Carry on!' he prompted. 'I find this interesting.'

'What else can I say?' she appealed, smiling. 'Except that I believe an intelligent person can never be bored.'

'Very true!' he agreed, giving a quick little nod of agreement. 'You assume, of course' — he went on, with a trace of laughter in his voice — 'that you possess a modicum of intelligence?'

'*Touché!*' she admitted, smiling. 'I'm not really so conceited as I sound.'

He smiled disarmingly. 'I don't think you are, Ruth. Well, if you don't want entertainment, or party tricks — perhaps you'd like me to make love to you?'

Ruth flushed, and looked away from the twinkle in his eyes.

'As you said, I'm different,' she countered. 'I don't want that either.'

'Pity!' he said quickly. 'I was beginning to look forward to the prospect.' She glanced at him swiftly, but he was smiling impishly.

'You must say that to every girl,' she teased and he laughed.

'The usual hackneyed phrase! I'm surprised at you, Ruth. I thought you could do better than that.'

Ruth said shyly: 'I suppose you wonder what I do want — why I came . . . ?' He shook his head.

'I never question any gift the Gods care to send me,' he assured her. 'I'm only too glad you did come. I was feeling depressed — and you arrived to cheer me up, in answer to a prayer.'

Ruth laughed into his eyes. 'I'm flattered! I've been called many things, but never 'a gift of the Gods' before!'

'Anyway' — he paused, suddenly curious — 'since you brought the subject up, why did you come to see me?' he asked. Ruth hesitated. 'Well?' he prompted.

'I simply wanted to see you,' she replied at last, a little shy. She looked down at her hands. He put his hand under her chin and lifted her face so that their eyes met.

'A remarkably good reason. I'm surprised at your interest in me, though,' he replied gallantly. For the first time he noticed an expression of cynicism in her candid grey eyes.

'I wonder? Don't you rather expect interest from every woman?'

'Do I give you that impression?' he countered. Ruth could not in all truth say that he did.

She shook her head. 'I'm sorry, Anton. That wasn't a very nice thing to say.'

'I agree with you,' he said, but he smiled. Gently, still keeping his hands cupped under her chin, he lowered his head and kissed her lips gently, so that it was a mere whisper of a kiss. Her lips parted under his, and he was tempted to linger, but he raised his head after a brief moment. 'Will you marry me, Ruth?' he heard himself saying. Although it had been his intention, he had not meant to spring it on the girl so abruptly, yet his heart had said it for him.

Ruth felt the colour rush into her face: her heart leaped with joy. For a moment she could not find words, she was filled with such emotion. It was the one thing she had longed for since she had met Anton, but had never really expected to hear. It couldn't be true that he had just asked her to marry him. This was all a wonderful but fantastic dream, and surely in a moment she would waken — and Anton would have eluded her again, as in so many of her dreams. She wanted to marry him more than anything in the world, but dared she take his proposal seriously. He sounded serious enough.

'Do you mean this, Anton?' she said breathlessly, and waited with agonizing pain for him to laugh and shake his head. But he didn't. Instead, he drew her into his arms and put his cheek close to hers.

'Yes, I mean it,' he assured her. 'I want you to marry me. Will you?' he asked again, and this time she nodded.

'Of course I will, Anton. I want to marry you so very much.' Saying this, she gave herself away completely. Anton knew in that moment that this young and lovely girl was deeply in love with him and he felt humbled, knowing that his reasons for asking her to marry him scarcely included love, although he felt a certain amount of affection for her.

He released her gently. 'Well, now you've said yes, how soon can you marry me?' Now that Anton had made up his mind, he was eager to act on his decision. She gave a little helpless gesture, not knowing what to say.

'Whenever you like, Anton.'

'How like a woman!' he laughed, getting to his feet. He went over to the mantelshelf and fumbled for his pipe, then as he carried on talking, he began to pack it from his pouch. 'Leave the decisions to the men!' he jeered with a smile.

'How about a fortnight to-day at eleven o'clock?'

'A *fortnight!*' Ruth gasped.

'Why not? Would you rather it was earlier?'

'No! I had no idea you meant it to be so soon . . . I expected a few months' engagement, at least.'

'It's unnecessary. We've decided to get married, so why waste time. I'll arrange everything. All you have to do is to be here on' — he glanced through his diary which lay on the mantelshelf — 'February 24th, at eleven a.m. We'll be married quietly at Caxton Hall.'

Ruth laughed a little helplessly. 'You have it all so cut and dried.'

'Why dither? I made up my mind

days ago — I only needed your confirmation. I think it will be quite a good arrangement, Ruth my dear.' He smiled across at her, then he suddenly sobered. 'Are you *sure*, Ruth? You don't want to go away and think about it — and then give me an answer? After all, there must be so many things you haven't stopped to consider. The fact that I'm fourteen years older than you, for one thing.'

'I don't think that's very important,' Ruth replied.

'It may not seem so now — but in later years . . . ' he paused as she shook her head. 'Well, if you're sure . . . '

'I am sure!' she said emphatically, and went over to him with a quick warm movement, putting her arms around him. He laid his cheek on her soft, shining hair.

'You will be happy, Ruth? I'd never forgive myself if you ever regretted marrying me.'

'As if I could,' she cried, straining up

to kiss his cheek. His arms tightened about her, and his lips brushed her hair, then he put her away from him. 'Come on, Ruth. I'll take you to lunch — we'll celebrate our engagement.'

4

When Ruth consented to marry Anton, she did not realize that he wanted the wedding to be a secret affair. She was rather dismayed when they discussed it over their celebration lunch. They had finished coffee and were idly smoking cigarettes when Anton suddenly leaned forward and laid his hand on hers.

'By the way, Ruth, there's one thing I must impress on you. Don't breathe a word to anyone about the wedding.'

'Why not, Anton?' she asked quickly.

'I want it to be kept absolutely quiet. We don't want all the newshounds on our trail, pestered by reporters and photographers for days to come, do we? You wouldn't like it, and I know that I don't. Anyway, Ruth, I can't really afford to lose my publicity value. As an eligible bachelor who is still in the marriage market, I'm good publicity — as a married man I'm not. D'you understand, my dear? It won't hurt *you*, it can't possibly matter to you very much.'

There was a sudden stricken look in her eyes, and she felt a pain grip her heart. She was quiet for a moment. To her it did matter, she wanted everyone to know how lucky she was in marrying Anton Radinov, but how could she make him understand that? After a moment she looked into his eyes and smiled warmly. If it was for his happiness and his pleasure, she would make any sacrifice. 'No, it doesn't matter,' she agreed. 'As long as I know I'm your wife, I don't mind, Anton.'

'Good girl!' he approved.

She left him in a confused state of mind. She knew she should be elated at the realization of her dreams, but the fact that she had to marry Anton secretly spoilt her elation. Dismayed, she wondered if the secrecy edict applied to her own family. Surely not? But Anton had insisted that no one must know. Her parents would be most upset if she married quietly, without telling them; disregarding all the pomp and ceremony of the white church wedding that they had always planned for her. But Anton came before her parents, much as she loved them. She felt in her heart that Anton would be a difficult man to live with. So far she had only known him socially — in fact she really didn't know him well at all. But she loved him. She would try to be tolerant of his moods — which he had warned her were very black and unpleasant — and perhaps in time she would understand him as fully as she now longed to do. As his wife, she had years before her to devote to making a success of their marriage. Anton had also told her that as his wife she would not be able to continue working at the advertising agency.

'I may be old fashioned,' he had smiled at her, 'but I insist on supporting my wife myself.' She had agreed; although she was happy at Gresham's Agency, it would be far more thrilling to work for Anton in their own home. She was looking forward to her wedding with joy and yet trepidation.

She only saw Anton twice between their day of their engagement and the wedding. The day following, she had gone to her home in Sussex for a few days. Her father, now recovered from his illness, had been glad to see her, and her mother, though worried a little about the general air of fragility surrounding Ruth and also the tiny hint of mystery in her daughter's plans for the future, had thoroughly enjoyed having her at home.

The day after she returned to London, she phoned Anton to tell him she was back. He immediately suggested that they should meet to buy her ring.

'You mean — go together to buy it?' Ruth asked.

'Of course. Why not? Or are you the

sentimental type who prefers surprises?'
he laughed.

'Yes,' she replied.

'You may not like my taste. No,
Ruth, you shall come with me,' he told
her decisively, and she had reluctantly
agreed.

So they met, and he selected a
beautiful diamond hoop ring for her.
Although Ruth looked over the rings, it
was Anton who made their final choice,
deciding that it was the perfect ring for
Ruth. That same evening they dined
and danced at a roadhouse just outside
London; Anton decided it was too risky
dining in a London restaurant where he
might so easily be recognized by friends
or journalists. He did not want Ruth's
name and photograph to be blazoned
across London's newspapers. He was
in an excellent mood, complimenting
Ruth lavishly, laughing with her and
generally showing her a light-hearted
side of himself that she had not known
he possessed.

Ruth arranged to dispose of her flat

to a girl friend conveniently in need of one, bought a small trousseau and generally straightened up her affairs. She left the agency, telling them that she was going back to Latimer to live, and spent the last week-end before her marriage sorting clothes and books. She thought with a little excitement of the lovely clothes she could buy once she was Anton's wife. It would be very pleasant to have plenty of money — though when she had agreed to marry him, she had not once thought of how rich or how famous he was. Though it would seem hard to believe, she thought with a little sigh, she was marrying him for no other reason than because she loved him.

When she finally woke on her wedding day, she ran quickly to her window, thinking of the old adage *'happy the bride the sun shines on'*. But February 24th had dawned cold and grey, dark clouds threatened and rain was imminent. So this was her wedding day — so different from all her dreams.

She supposed it was natural to feel nervous, but she hoped she would be more composed during the actual ceremony, which she knew would be very brief and cold. She loved Anton and wanted nothing more than to marry him: she longed to be his wife and devote her life to making him happy — so why be nervous? she chided herself as she dressed. Of course she experienced doubts: what young bride did not? Was she doing the right thing; should she marry a man who was almost a stranger; would she make him happy; was it possible that she could be the right sort of wife for him? These and like questions ran through her brain. She did not ask herself if Anton loved her — she naturally assumed that he would not have wanted to marry her if he didn't love her, although he had never declared any love for her.

She took a taxi to his flat. She hastened up the stairs and rang the bell, shivering a little from nervousness and excitement. Impatient, she rang again.

No sooner had she done so than the door opened abruptly and she looked up into a stranger's face. Gregg smiled down at her reassuringly.

Ruth thought fleetingly that he was very tall, taller even than Anton, with very broad shoulders tapering to slim hips. He was immaculately dressed. In a quick glance, Ruth noted his proudly held head, the fiery auburn hair and the kind, reassuring blue eyes that smiled down at her.

'You must be Ruth,' he said quickly. 'Please come in. I couldn't mistake you after hearing Anton's description.'

She smiled at him and went in.

Gregg closed the door then hurried to take her coat as she slipped it from her shoulders.

'I'm Gregg Randall,' he told her.

Ruth gave him the pale blue light-weight coat. Beneath it she wore a silver grey suit with pale blue gloves and tiny hat, silver grey shoes and handbag. She looked very lovely. Excitement had heightened her natural colour and made her eyes bright. She went into the lounge, expecting to find Anton, but the room was empty.

She turned enquiringly to Gregg. 'Where's Anton?'

'He won't be long — he's dressing,' Gregg told her. He grinned. 'Did you think he had escaped your clutches at the last minute?'

Ruth shook her head, smiling faintly. She crossed to the windows and glanced out, a little shy of this stranger. She wished Anton had been there to greet her, and to give her the assurance that everything would be all right.

'Anton asked me to look after you. Will you have a drink?' Gregg crossed to the cabinet and she turned, pensive, to watch him as he poured drinks for them both.

'Dutch courage?' she asked, smiling.

'Yes, if that's what you need.' Gregg handed her a sweet sherry and she accepted it with a smile of approval at his choice. Gregg gave her a cigarette, lighting it for her from the table-lighter.

Ruth bent her head over the flame, trying to control her trembling fingers. Gregg sat down in a deep armchair, quite at home, crossing one leg over the other, his drink in his hand. He smiled up at her. 'Feeling nervous?'

Ruth nodded. 'A little,' she admitted.

'Mm. I thought so. Very natural in the circumstances. A girl doesn't get married every day.' He indicated the settee. 'Won't you sit down and relax?' She nodded and sat down, first stubbing out her cigarette. After a moment, Gregg went on. 'Anton is so cool about the whole thing that he makes me feel perfectly unnecessary.'

'Unnecessary?' Ruth raised her eyebrows. 'Why?'

'Well, you see — I'm the best man. At least, I would be if this were the normal sort of affair. As it is, I'm a mere witness. I'm supposed to boost Anton's morale, keep his courage up and ensure his arrival at the altar, but he doesn't seem to need my services at all. Most disheartening!'

Ruth smiled. 'Then — if you will — perhaps you'll devote your talents to boosting my morale instead. I'm terrified!'

Gregg nodded. 'You look composed, but that doesn't mean a thing.' He paused, then went on. 'You haven't known Anton long, have you?'

Ruth shook her head. 'Not very long. About six weeks, I suppose.'

'Yes, that's what I thought,' Gregg nodded. He was remembering Anton's comments to him on this marriage and they didn't please him. Studying this sweet and rather shy young girl, he decided that Anton was being unnecessarily ruthless; if anyone suffered from this hasty marriage — as no doubt they would — it would certainly not be Anton. He felt rather grim as he continued: 'Look, far be it from me to interfere in your personal life, Ruth — you don't mind if I call you that . . . ?' he broke off to ask, then as she shook her head, 'Good! I presume you're old enough to know what you're

83

doing, but I hope you've considered this marriage very carefully.' Ruth stiffened, flushing at his presumption.

'Thank you, yes! It may seem crazy to you that we want to be married so soon after meeting each other, but it doesn't take long to fall in love. We want to get married — and it didn't take much consideration on either side to know it's the right thing.'

'You're annoyed!' Gregg stated. 'I'm not really surprised — it's very presumptuous of me, I know, but as Anton and I are good friends, I hope you'll forgive me.' She had confirmed his suspicions. Ruth imagined that Anton was in love with her. She obviously loved him. Gregg felt a sudden pity for her, knowing that whatever it was that had prompted Anton to marry this girl, love did not come into it. It was not up to him to disillusion Ruth; that would come with time, but he wished he could spare her the certain ensuing grief and disappointment. He felt a deep sympathy for her. He hoped she would find the happiness she was seeking in her marriage, but he very much doubted if she would. Anton was far too selfish and arrogant to make a very satisfactory husband.

Ruth forgave him willingly. She did not bear grudges at any time, least of all on her wedding day, the most exciting day of her life. 'Have you known Anton very long?' she asked, politely.

'Four years or so,' Gregg replied, just as politely. 'We were in *Laughing Criminal* together — d'you remember it? — it had a very good run, which isn't surprising with Anton in the star role. He's an astonishingly good actor, you know — but don't tell him I said so — he's conceited enough!' They laughed together.

'I've not met an actor yet who wasn't conceited,' Ruth teased him.

'*Touché!*' Gregg conceded. 'We can't help it, you know. Mass adulation is bound to go to one's head.'

'Depends on the strength of one's head,' retorted Ruth.

'Well, Anton's isn't very strong. One dose of flattery and he's bowled over immediately!' Gregg warned her, smiling.

'You think that's what happened with us?' she asked. He shrugged, grinning.

'Who knows what form a woman's wiles will take?'

Anton could hear their laughter as he dressed and he wondered at the subject of their conversation. He entered the room in time to hear Gregg's last remark, striding across the room with a smile.

'Hallo, my dear. Has Gregg been looking after you competently?' He bent down to touch her cheek with his finger caressingly, then crossed to pour himself a drink.

'Naturally. I'm always competent,' Gregg replied quickly before Ruth could speak.

'Yes, thank you, Anton,' Ruth said,

smiling across at him a trifle shyly. Sudden joy surged in her as their eyes met. How handsome, how wonderful he was! — this man who was so soon to be her husband.

'Good! Everything is in order. The wedding is at eleven, as I said, Ruth, and I've arranged lunch at Adano's to follow. How does that appeal?'

'Jolly good! My favourite restaurant,' commended Gregg. 'Do you know it, Ruth?'

'No,' she admitted. 'I've never been there.'

'Then you have an adventure in store,' Anton told her gaily. He felt very light of heart to-day. He had not imagined that his wedding day could afford him so much pleasure in anticipation and experience. He was quite happy about this marriage — once his mind was made up, he seldom changed his decisions. How lovely Ruth was looking, he mused, studying her with approval. She certainly dressed beautifully. That suit looked as if it had cost the earth . . .

Ruth was pleased to note his good humour, his obvious air of happiness. Instantly the day did not seem so dull and grey. How boyish he could be, she thought, how lovable when his blue eyes laughed into hers, dancing with mischief.

'By the way, I've a present for you, Ruth.' Anton crossed to the table by the door. He came back with a cellophane box and handed it to her. Ruth gazed at the contents. The loveliest orchid she had ever seen lay on its velvet base.

'How beautiful!' she exclaimed involuntarily. 'Anton, this is wonderful!'

'I'm glad you like it. Every bride should wear flowers. Here, let me pin it on for you.'

Ruth took the flower from its box and with Anton's help it was soon fastened to her lapel. Gregg watched the pair, fascinated by Ruth's youthful air of naïvety and her candid sweetness. She was so transparently honest and unaffected. Gregg found a vast difference in her to the usual women friends that Anton escorted around town, who were so blasé as to be painful, and would have scorned to show pleasure or excitement over such a simple offering. Gregg hoped that Ruth would be a good influence on Anton, though he doubted whether anyone could change Anton at this late hour. But perhaps she could soften that hard core of bitterness in him, draw out his natural charm and tenderness, transform him from a hard, cynical, embittered rake into a gentle, loving and unselfish man.

Gregg looked at his watch. 'If we don't hurry, you two won't be getting married to-day. Like time and tide, registrars wait for no man!'

During the drive to Caxton Hall, Anton was buoyant and talkative, but Ruth sat quiet, pale and trembling a little. Gregg let Anton ramble on, occasionally replying to his remarks, but he was afraid for Ruth's sudden pallor. Sitting beside her, he could sense her body trembling. He felt pity for her and a warmth ran through his veins as he reached out his hand and gripped hers reassuringly, glad to note an answering pressure. He met her eyes and smiled warmly. She smiled tremulously in return, but she was still white-faced. Anton seemed oblivious to Ruth's silence or her pallor and Gregg felt sudden anger. He fought to control the blazing current of anger that swept over him.

'You're looking grim,' Anton remarked, catching sight of his friend's face in the driving mirror. 'What's wrong?'

'Nothing at all,' Gregg replied swiftly. 'What should be wrong?'

'I thought perhaps you were nervous,' Anton laughed. 'Isn't it usual for the groom to face the ordeal with calm fortitude while the best man shakes in his shoes? — by the way, I hope you've got the wedding ring safe in your pocket.'

Gregg patted his breast pocket. 'Quite safe.'

Anton brought the car to an abrupt stop outside Caxton Hall, then looked at his watch. 'We've about five or six minutes in hand. Gregg, you take Ruth in — keep a firm hold on her. I'm not really sure that she won't change her mind at the last minute.' He grinned at Ruth, obviously quite confident that it was the last thing she would do. 'I'll park the car round the corner.'

'How do I know *you* won't change your mind — and not come back?' Ruth asked, smiling as their eyes met in the driving mirror. He turned in his seat to look at her warmly.

'I shall be with you in a few minutes, Ruth,' he assured her.

'He'd be a fool not to turn up,' Gregg said to Ruth. 'But if he doesn't, you'll simply have to marry me, that's all. We can't do the registrar out of a wedding!'

The ceremony was brief and Ruth scarcely felt as though she had actually been married to Anton. Just a few mumbled words, a wide gold band slipped on her finger and she was Mrs. Anton Radinov — just like that!! As they came out of Caxton Hall, Ruth fingered the gold band wonderingly. Gregg noticed and touched her elbow briefly, gently.

'It's quite true, Ruth. You really are married.'

'Yes, the foul deed is done,' exclaimed Anton as he caught up with them. He had remained behind to tip the clerk, who was their second witness, and the registrar.

'I suggest a drink,' Gregg said. 'We must toast the bride.'

'Good idea!' commended Anton. They found a tiny pub round the corner and drank each other's health. Ruth, now the actual ceremony was over, felt far more at ease and less shy of Gregg after his kind support. Colour soon came back to her cheeks, her eyes began to shine and she was soon bandying words with the pair of them. It was a merry toasting. Anton made every effort to be charming to Ruth, more in an endeavour to show Gregg that he would make her happy than to please his bride.

Adano's was an exclusive, continental restaurant with soft lighting, intimate seating and deferential waiters. They had a delightful lunch, beautifully cooked and served. Ruth looked around with interest, admiring the long gleaming bar, the lovely decorated mirror panel running the length of one wall, the deep, luxurious carpeting, the shaded, attractive lighting that gave the room its rosy glow. Ruth sat spellbound listening to the two men talking, telling her of their theatrical lives and experiences. It was a glimpse into another world for Ruth.

Gregg promised he would call on Ruth frequently, when Anton was busy at the theatre, so that she would not be too lonely. 'That is, if you'll have me?' he added, with a warm smile.

'I shall love to see you,' she responded quickly, her eyes smiling at him. He was charming. Such good company and so sympathetic.

'I don't suppose Anton has told you that his flat is almost my second home — you'll never be rid of me, especially now he has such a delightful wife!' Gregg told her. Their eyes met and held for one long moment, then Ruth dropped her eyes.

'Hey! Are you trying to cut me out?' Anton asked quickly, tapping Gregg on the shoulder and giving a mock frown.

'No . . . not yet. But it's not such a bad idea,' Gregg returned.

Ruth laughed. 'I don't think you'll be very successful,' she told him.

'I should think not!' exclaimed Anton. 'I think we'd better go, Ruth, before Gregg makes any more advances. He's almost holding your hand now, right under my very eyes. I shudder to think what he'll be up to when I'm not around!'

Gregg laughed. He took out his wallet and placed the necessary money on the tray, covering the bills. 'As it's your wedding day, I'll settle the bill,' he said. 'But don't make a habit of getting married, Anton, it might work out expensive!'

5

Ruth hummed merrily as she went from one part of the room to the other, dusting. She wore a gay little dress of cherry-red cotton piped with white, and white sandals. The sunshine streamed in through the long mullioned window that ran the length of one wall and lit up the room with bright rays, the dust rising to gleam in the sunlight. Ruth felt a sweet feeling of possession steal through her as she looked around her home — their home. She and Anton had been married for six weeks already and to-day Ruth felt wonderfully happy.

Anton was very complex. One day he would be gay, mischievous, brimming with personality and Ruth would worship him; the next day he might wake depressed, bitter, black of mood and nothing would please him. He would snarl at Ruth, pace the flat restlessly, criticizing everything and eventually fling out of the flat in a vicious temper, leaving her alone for hours — and, on two or three occasions, overnight. Ruth would worry almost to the point of illness. On these occasions, when he returned he was exceptionally sweet and repentant.

Ruth was alone in the flat at the moment. Anton was lunching with his agent, Flavek. A decision was to be made with regard to the new play at the Atheneum Theatre in the autumn. At the moment, Anton was still in the cast of *A Question of Murder?* but his plans for leaving were well advanced. Ruth understood that Anton had many calls on his time, but she wished that he didn't have to leave her alone quite so much. She occupied her time for the most part with housework, having got rid of Anton's daily woman. This had been against Anton's wishes, but Ruth had insisted that she must do something with her days.

Anton's wedding present to her was a blue Siamese kitten and Ruth found Yasmin to be a welcome companion. But Yasmin could not talk and Ruth was lonely.

At present, Anton's mood was gay and affectionate, and it was because of this that Ruth hummed happily and surveyed the flat with contentment shining in her eyes. Before the change of mood, he had indulged in a perverse fit of cynicism, making Ruth quite miserable. She depended on him completely for her happiness. She worried over his moods and was afraid of them. It was this that made Anton speak even sharper to her and be deliberately perverse: if she had ignored his moods, they certainly wouldn't have lasted so long. Ruth plumped up a cushion, leant to stroke Yasmin and then picked up Anton's beloved pipe that he had left on the table. For a brief moment, she held it to her cheek, because it was something of Anton. She was so hungry for his love — she knew now deep in her heart that he didn't love her, but she would not admit it. During the past weeks, the fact that Anton was not in love with her had become apparent to the sensitive, loving girl. She yearned suddenly for the touch of his lips, the embrace of his arms and she wished he were home.

As though in answer to her silent wish, the doorbell pealed. Had Anton forgotten his key? she wondered, hurrying to the door. She flung it wide, her eyes shining, her lips parted in a welcoming smile. Gregg stood grinning down at her from his bronzed height. She hadn't seen him since her wedding day and now, remembering his kindness to her, she was delighted to see him. 'Come in, Gregg!' she welcomed. 'I'm so glad to see you.'

'I'm sorry I'm not Anton,' he apologized, smiling. She raised an enquiring eyebrow. 'I'm sure that warm reception was meant for your husband.'

Ruth flushed. 'Yes. I did think it was Anton. We don't have visitors, you see.'

'I'm not a visitor. I told you, this is my second home. How are you, Ruth?'

'Wonderful! I feel fine.' She led the way into the lounge.

'You look as if you're loving life,' he commented, taking out his cigarettes and offering her the case. She shook her head in refusal.

'Sit down, Gregg. I'll make you some tea — or do you prefer coffee? I'm not much use with the percolator,' she smiled apologetically. 'Anton always makes the coffee.'

'Very domesticated of him. I'll have tea, please.' He followed her into the tiny kitchen.

'Gregg, why haven't you come before? I've been hoping to see you,' she told him, busying herself with cups.

'Have you?' He lounged in the doorway, watching her set tea-things on a tray. 'I thought I'd give you a few weeks to get used to married life.'

'Sweet of you!' She flashed him a laughing glance, then as the kettle rattled for attention, turned back to her task. Gregg watched her. She looked well and very happy. Was he wrong after all in imagining Anton to be a difficult husband? Was it possible that Anton loved this girl? Gregg could imagine it would be very easy to fall in love with Ruth, but Anton was a strange man. The sun shone through the window, and gleamed on her dancing golden curls. Her eyes sparkled — she looked completely in love with life! Or was it simply being in love with Anton that made her look so radiant? Gregg knew that the image of Ruth had nestled in his heart ever since her wedding day — since her marriage to his best friend — and this was the real reason why he had avoided his friend's home for so long.

'Really happy, Ruth?' he asked gently, taking the tray from her. For a moment, they looked into each other's eyes, as he blocked her way into the lounge. She nodded shyly. 'All the time?' he pressed and did not miss the sudden shadow that flitted across her face.

'Yes, of course,' she said quickly, a trifle too quickly. Gregg sighed. He carried the tray into the lounge and laid it on the low coffee table. As he did so, he caught sight of Yasmin.

'What a lovely cat!' he exclaimed.

'She's beautiful, isn't she? Anton gave her to me as a wedding present. She's called Yasmin.'

Gregg stroked the kitten, who sleepily opened her eyes, gave him the once-over, then, satisfied, went back to sleep. Gregg turned away from the cat, sat down by Ruth and took the cup she handed him. He stirred his tea idly.

'Tell me, Ruth, what do you do with yourself all day?' he asked, smiling at her.

'Anton's out most of the time . . . ' Ruth began.

'I know that. I want to know what

you do,' Gregg reminded her gently and she smiled.

'I'm busy with housework — does that surprise you? It does Anton. He never expected me to be that sort of wife.' She laughed. 'I tell him that I must have something to occupy me. Then I have Yasmin — and reading. When Anton's in, we play records and talk. Of course, he has a lot of luncheons and dinner parties to attend and all the other things that go with being a successful actor — not that I have to tell *you* what they are — ' she broke off, smiling.

'It isn't much fun for you,' he said quietly, disregarding the compliment. 'Nor can it be very easy being married to a man like Anton.'

'Oh, he's difficult at times,' she conceded. 'I should think all men are. But he can be charming and very kind.'

'You think that's enough?' he said in astonishment.

'Oh, he's affectionate too, and very

sensible,' she went on, unobservant of the effect her words had on Gregg. He was amazed to find how little she expected of the man she had married, the man she believed was in love with her. 'I'm sure he doesn't mean to get annoyed with me, as he does sometimes,' she continued, 'perhaps I'm the type of woman who gets on people's nerves all unconsciously.'

'You don't get on mine,' Gregg assured her, smiling.

'But you don't live with me,' she pointed out, laughing up at him. 'I expect I can be very annoying.'

'You're very loyal, anyway. But I suppose it's understandable. You haven't been married long — and you love him very much, don't you?'

'Am I being cross-examined?' she laughed.

Quickly he apologized. 'I'm sorry. I don't mean to be rude.'

'You're not,' she assured him. 'Yes, I do love Anton very much. Do you blame me?'

His eyes darkened suddenly. 'Blame you? Yes, I do . . . What is there to love in him? What is there about him that makes the women fall at his feet? He's arrogant, selfish, bad-tempered . . .' he broke off, noticing her sudden pallor.

'Go on!' she said softly, icily. 'Do let me hear what his *friend* thinks of my husband.'

Gregg put down his cup and turned towards her, laying his hand on hers gently. 'I'm sorry, Ruth. I shouldn't have said such things to you. Believe me, I didn't mean to hurt you.' She withdrew her hand pointedly, still angry with him. The coldness of her eyes and the gesture pained him. 'You're angry with me,' he said wryly. 'I always seem to say the wrong thing to you.' She did not answer. She did not understand his bitterness against Anton. She had believed him a friend, and he had turned against the man she loved. 'Ruth!' he said softly, 'I'm damned fond of Anton, you know that. You're thinking that because I said such things,

I must *think* them. Perhaps I do! I may condemn Anton for what he is, but that doesn't change my affection for him. I said to you he is arrogant, selfish, bad-tempered — do you believe I tell that to the world in general? Do you believe I call myself his friend and criticize him behind his back to all and sundry? If you do, then I won't annoy you any longer with my company.' He got to his feet, hurt that she didn't detain him. She looked up at him, wanting to keep him with her yet still angry: his words had not softened her feelings. As they stood looking at each other in a still moment, the front door slammed and Anton came into the room.

'Why, hallo! Gregg! This is grand. How are you? You haven't been near us for weeks, where have you been all this time?' Gregg turned to shake Anton's hand warmly. They clasped hands, Anton resting his other hand for a moment on Gregg's shoulder in a warm grasp. 'Ruth, weren't you pleased to see Gregg?'

'Yes, of course.' She replied softly, smiling tenderly at him, but she was angrier still that Gregg could greet Anton so warmly after being so cutting about him. 'Tea, Anton? I've just made some.'

'Good! I've been talking my tongue loose this afternoon — arguing with Flavek. He doesn't think we should risk this new play — just because it's an unknown author. As I told him, all of us are unknowns to start with. I told him I'm determined, I have faith in this play — if he isn't happy about it, I can always get another agent. That scared the pants off him! He daren't lose me!' Anton sat down in his favourite chair, groping for the pipe that usually laid on the arm. He leaned forward to take the cup Ruth offered him, as Gregg sat down again beside Ruth.

'I was just going, Anton,' he said.

'Going? Good God, man, going without seeing me? What is this, a *tête-à-tête* with my wife?' Anton grinned, then frowned as he failed to find his pipe. 'Ruth, where's my pipe? Have you moved it?'

She jumped up. 'Here it is, Anton.' She retrieved the pipe swiftly from the mantelshelf and handed it to him. He smiled at her.

'Thanks. What were you two talking about when I came in? You looked very intense!'

'Did we?' Gregg smiled. 'I can't remember. I don't think it was important.'

'It wasn't,' Ruth said quickly.

'It's a glorious day — so warm. Unusual for so early in April,' Anton said absentmindedly, lighting his pipe.

'I hope it's like this for Easter,' Ruth said, smiling at her husband.

'Mm,' he grunted. 'Pity I'm still tied up with the Venus play. If I was out of that we could have had that honeymoon you're still waiting for.' Ruth flushed slightly as Anton smiled across at her.

'I thought you were soon leaving the Venus,' Gregg said, leaning forward to light his cigarette from Anton's match.

'It's still under discussion. Anyway, Ruth, I promise I'll take you somewhere on Easter Sunday. We can go for a trip to the sea in the old jalopy, if you like. Perhaps Gregg would come with us,' he glanced at Gregg enquiringly. 'Are you free?' Gregg looked swiftly at Ruth. Was she still angry with him? How was she taking this invitation? She did not meet his eyes, afraid that her own would betray her. Much as she liked Gregg, she welcomed the prospect of a day alone with Anton, their first day out together.

'Don't worry about Ruth. She'd love you to come with us,' Anton spoke for his wife.

'I'll let you know. I'm not really sure of my movements at the moment,' Gregg said, hesitantly, only waiting for Ruth to add her persuasions to Anton's.

'Ring me when you decide. I think I'm free . . . ' A sudden thought struck

Anton. He leaped to his feet with a characteristic, graceful movement and sought his little leather book in which he noted all his engagements. 'I'd better check.' He leafed through the pages. 'What date is Easter . . . Ah, here it is; 17th April is Good Friday, isn't it? Sunday, the 19th. Damn! I'm tied up. I promised to go to Kerry Moore's house-party that week-end — I shall have to go.' He turned and flashed a quick, apologetic smile at Ruth. 'Sorry about that, my dear.'

'Must you go, Anton?' Ruth protested, disappointed. 'Surely not Easter . . . ?' Anton came over to her, sat down on the arm of the settee and slipped his arm round her shoulders to give her a brief hug.

'I'm sorry, Ruth. When I made this promise, I didn't know I'd have you to consider by Easter. It's a long-standing date.'

'Can't you write or phone and say you can't go?' Ruth pleaded, relaxing against him. He ruffled her short curls with a caressing hand.

'I don't break promises, sweet. In any case, there'll be a crowd of my friends and I shall probably enjoy myself.'

'But what will *I* do?' Ruth's lips trembled suddenly, her heart filled with disappointment and, she knew, a slight resentment at Anton's unconcern for her.

'I know,' Anton said slowly. 'It isn't very nice for you.' He paused, then looked at Gregg. 'I say, Gregg, will you look after Ruth that week-end — if you *are* free?'

Gregg returned his glance, an inscrutable expression in his eyes. Ruth raised her head proudly, almost arrogantly.

'Gregg doesn't want to be bothered with me,' she said quickly. 'Don't be silly, Anton. I'll go home for the week-end.'

'Home?' Anton looked at her enquiringly.

'My parents' home. I haven't seen them for some time. They'll love to have me for a few days.'

'Well, that's solved the problem. It will be nicer for you than being here on your own, anyway, Ruth.' Anton sat back, relieved that the whole thing had been settled satisfactorily.

'Perhaps I could drive you, Ruth?' Gregg leaned forward eagerly. 'Anton will be too busy, I expect. When will you go?'

'I don't know. It's very kind of you, Gregg, but I expect I shall go by train. Probably on the Thursday. I needn't come back until late Monday or early Tuesday, need I, Anton?'

Anton frowned. 'I don't know that I want you to be away quite so long, Ruth. I'm not going away myself until after Saturday's performance, and I suppose I'm used now to having you around.' He smiled disarmingly.

'Is it necessary for Ruth to kick her heels here for those couple of days?' Gregg asked.

'Oh, I don't mind,' Ruth said quickly, glad of Anton's need of her.

'It really doesn't make any difference. I can go home on Saturday.'

'In that case, may I drive you down *then*?' Gregg asked, still pressing the matter.

'Can I let you know?' Ruth returned. 'I haven't made up my mind what to do yet.' She laughed. 'I may not even go home at all.'

Gregg nodded. Ruth stood and picked up the tea-tray. Gregg leaped up. 'Let me take that!'

'No. I can manage, thanks.' Ruth smiled at him, then leaving the two men to talk, she went into the kitchen. When she returned, some time later, both men were laughing. Anton was gay and cheerful and the shadow had left Gregg's eyes. They turned and smiled as she came in.

'You were a long time,' Anton commented. Ruth smiled but did not answer and the two men returned to their discussion. She picked up Yasmin, who stretched luxuriously in her arms. She stood cuddling the

113

kitten, resting her cheek against its coat. Yasmin began to purr contentedly. Ruth went over to the window and stood looking out, thoughtfully. She was still uncertain what to do about Easter. To Ruth, Easter had always seemed important: the time for new clothes, summery things, a fresh, revitalized outlook. She was young and in love with life — and life at the moment represented Anton to her. She longed to be with him, somewhere on their own, away from the town and the constant fear that reporters would discover their secret marriage. She had been hoping that the Easter week-end would mean a few days away with Anton. She did not want to go home: her parents were sure to notice how much she had changed since they last saw her and her mother was sure to worm the secret of her wedding to Anton out of her — and Anton had made her swear not to tell anyone! It was very hard not to tell her mother things.

Gregg came and stood behind her: Anton was looking up a book for him amongst his collection. 'You're miles away, aren't you?' he said softly, teasingly. She turned unseeing eyes on him, then recognition dawned.

'Sorry, Gregg. I was dreaming. What did you say?'

He laughed. 'It doesn't matter. Are you still wild with me, Ruth?' She met his eyes which pleaded for forgiveness, filled with gentle affection and remorse. She shook her head.

'No. I'm not angry now.'

'Will you let me drive you to your parents' home?' he urged.

'Oh, Gregg, don't press me,' she protested. 'I don't know what to do with the week-end.'

'You're disappointed,' he defined softly. 'I'm sorry.'

She shrugged. 'It can't be helped. I'm just a minor detail in Anton's life — naturally he has other things to do!'

'Don't be bitter, Ruth,' he said

quickly. 'It's unlike you. Don't let Anton make you unhappy or bitter.'

She smiled. 'I'm sorry. I think living with a cynic has something to do with it.'

'You mustn't change at all, Ruth. You're sweet as you are.' He went on swiftly: 'Look . . . let me take you out at Easter. Anton won't mind. He's going away. We could go to the sea on Sunday — perhaps the Zoo or Windsor or racing on Monday. How would you like that?'

Her eyes lit up. 'Lovely! It would be nice, Gregg. D'you think Anton will raise any objections?'

'Why should he? It was his suggestion — not that he influenced me,' he added hurriedly. She smiled.

'I believe you. All right, Gregg. It's a very good idea and I shall love to go with you.'

'I'm only second-best,' he teased, grinning. 'But I hope you'll enjoy yourself with me.' She laughed with him. Anton came to join them with a book in his hand.

'Here you are, Gregg. Read this and tell me if I wasn't right.'

Gregg took the book, open at the desired page and began to read, Anton watching him and waiting for his comments. Ruth stroked Yasmin's back gently, glad that some definite plan was formed for the Easter week-end.

★ ★ ★

Anton listened to her recital of the arrangements as he undressed that night in their room. She was brushing her hair in front of the dressing-table, a loose gown about her shoulders, her eyes starry with excitement.

'It seems as if you intend to enjoy yourself,' he commented, when she paused for breath. She turned and looked at him quickly as he buttoned his pyjama coat.

'Do you mind, Anton? Are you angry?'

He went across and kissed her

forehead. 'Of course not, silly. I'm glad that you won't be moping here. Gregg is a splendid companion.'

'I wish I could be with you,' she said simply and put her arms round him. He let her hold him for a few seconds, then he released himself.

'Never mind, Ruth.' He bent to drop a kiss on her curls then went to brush his teeth. Ruth looked after him, her heart in her eyes. When he returned, she was in bed, lying on her back with her arms under her head, her eyes still starry. Anton looked down on her, wondering what she was thinking and whether the stars in her eyes were for him. He sat down on her bed and put his arms about her. She smiled at him tremulously. 'You lovely creature,' he murmured and kissed her. She clung to him, revelling in the strength of his arms, the pressure of his lips. When he drew away, she pulled him back and he laid his cheek against hers. She caressed his head, love surging through her. Passionate words of love fought for utterance, but shy, she did not speak them — not only shyness but fear of a rebuff held her back. Anton could sense the tide of love that he had aroused in her.

'I wish you didn't love me so much,' he whispered, and was surprised, for he had not meant to say the words. She held him even closer.

'I can't help it, darling,' she said gently. 'I just do.' She clung to him suddenly and he held her close. 'Oh, Anton, Anton . . .' she cried. He soothed her gently. The desperate cry was born of longing for his love.

'Darling, what's the matter?' he asked her as he felt tears on her cheeks. 'Tell me, Ruth.' She was startled by the endearment, the first sincere one, she felt, that he had spoken. She shook her head wordlessly. How could she tell him that she longed for him to love her? How could she explain?

'Well, don't cry then, my little one,' he murmured. 'It doesn't matter if you can't tell me. I understand.' He kissed her and was shaken by her eager response. What depths of love this child possessed! He wondered why he could not love her in return. Perhaps a man was incapable of this intensity of feeling — he could not remember ever having felt such emotion for any woman. He was naturally fond of Ruth, she was so very sweet, she made him a good wife and he appreciated her efforts, but he did wish that she would not look for love from him — at least, love in the way that she meant and obviously felt. He released her. 'Come, let me go, Ruth,' he chided gently as she clutched his hand. 'I'm tired, sweet.'

'Stay with me,' she pleaded. He grinned, teasingly, and ruffled her hair.

'Go to sleep, you temptress!'

'I don't feel sleepy,' she smiled.

'You never do,' he reminded her, laughing. She lay looking up at him, her eyes shining.

'I adore you, Anton!'

'That won't get you anywhere,' he told her in mock reproof. 'It's twenty to one, child, and I'm tired.' She raised herself to kiss his chin. He laughed and pulled her to him. 'I surrender! I'll stay with you. Kiss me, Ruth!' Willingly, she gave him her lips.

6

Anton turned his head to smile at Rona. She sat beside him in his new white sports car, the breeze ruffling her hair, her eyes sparkling with excitement. Glancing at her now, he again felt the thrill of physical longing, the sudden spark of desire that always gripped him when he was with her.

On this lovely Easter Sunday, with the hot sun blazing down, Ruth was forgotten. Anton had arrived in the early hours of the morning, after driving down from town when the Saturday performance was over, free for a couple of days. The whole house had been blazing with lights, his friends hurrying out to meet him at the sound of his car, awaiting his arrival with unconcealed warmth. Kerry and Nadia, his young wife, greeted him warmly: close behind stood Rona, her eager acceptance of his brief kiss had stirred him. He had known that Rona would be there: perhaps this knowledge had been his reason for refusing to cancel his arrangements. Her beautiful expectant eyes turned towards him, the lovely flame of her hair glowing against her milky shoulders and the obvious happiness she felt at his arrival had all helped to increase his desire for her.

Now they sped down the coast road to the private bay that Kerry owned, a noisy carload of young people close behind. The cool breeze caused by the speed of the car was very welcome.

Rona, dressed in a green bathing-suit, had slung a short white coat over her shoulders; her long, brown legs were bare and attractive. The bathing-suit did nothing to hide her curvaceous figure nor did it help Anton to keep his mind on the road.

Kerry Moore was a charming, pleasant-faced man of about forty-four or so, who had been well established in films for about eight years: his wife was the very lovely film starlet of seventeen, Nadia Norris, and they had been married only a few months. The brief thought flashed through Anton's mind that it was quite usual these days for a young girl to marry a man so much older than herself — and he remembered with a wry grin that he was fourteen years older than Ruth.

But Ruth was far from his thoughts at the moment. Rona was too close! He knew that Rona had been invited for his benefit — it was common knowledge that they were deep in an affair. The other members of the houseparty were two young starlet friends of Nadia's and their current men friends; Barry Preston (an actor of some note who, with Anton, was being considered as a lead for the new play) and his second wife, Ailsa, one of London's top models until her recent marriage; Jay Scott, the theatre critic whose satiric pen made even the most confident actor cautious; and Kerry's brother, Mark, who wrote detective novels with some success.

Anton drew into the bay, the other car following him. It was a lovely spot on the coast of Kent. Golden sands backed by white cliffs, miles from any other people, so that they could relax completely and be assured of privacy.

Within a few minutes, Anton and Rona were stretched out on the warm sand; Jill and Keith a little distance from them, while Nadia, Owen, Bill and Ailsa played with a beach ball farther away. Kerry was exercising his two large Alsatians on the cliff and waved to them; his brother Mark was with him.

Anton lay on his back, shielding his eyes from the sun. He was very conscious of Rona's body next to his own. Out of the corner of his eye he could see Keith bending over Jill, teasing her, biting her tiny ears and playing with her hair. He grinned to himself. Jill was a pretty, dark little thing with exciting black eyes — he could understand Keith's fascination.

'You look happy, darling. Are you?'

Rona rolled over on to her stomach and propped herself up on her elbows to look at him.

'Of course. It's nice to relax — don't you think so?'

'Mm!' After a moment, she went on: 'I'm glad you came, Anton. I wondered if you had forgotten this week-end — you didn't mention it when I saw you on Wednesday.' He had taken her to lunch during the week.

'Didn't I?' He grinned. 'Perhaps I wanted to surprise you — make you think I had forgotten.'

'You devil!' She leant over him and bit his ear, nipping the lobe between her small white teeth. He shouted in mock pain and gave her a resounding slap. Within seconds they were indulging in a pretty display of horseplay. Soon tiring, Anton lay back and let her pummel him without protest. She gave up the attempt and lay down beside him again, even closer this time and put her arm across his body.

'I want to get sunburnt, silly!' he

rebuked her, pushing her arm away. 'Do you think I want a white arm across a brown chest — what would my wife say?' His eyes laughed at her and she felt a thrill shoot through her. How handsome he was, a magnificent man.

'You haven't a wife!' she said quickly, 'at least, I think! I wouldn't put it past you to have one tucked away somewhere!' She was teasing him and he knew it, so he merely grinned slowly at her and pulled her to him. She went willingly, pressing her body against him as they kissed and slowly that pressure grew more passionate. At last he released her and drew a deep breath.

'What you do to my blood pressure is nobody's business! Be quiet for a while. You can't expect me to make love to you here.'

She laughed exultantly. As she lay back obediently, she looked even more desirable. 'I don't see why not. D'you think the others would mind?' She flashed him a provocative glance.

'That's not the point. I would! I have my modesty,' he fooled, twining his fingers in her long hair. He loved her hair. It was so long, such a beautiful colour and always so well groomed.

'Modesty!' she jeered. 'You don't know the meaning of the word!'

'You certainly don't,' he rejoined quickly, with a meaning glance at her very revealing swim-suit. She laughed.

'I thought you would appreciate my new suit. I bought it specially for you, darling.'

'Hussy! You would have worn it had I been here or not — simply to attract *men*, not one man, and you know it. Perhaps I shouldn't have come after all. You might easily have captivated Jay!'

'Jay!' she exclaimed sharply. 'That woman hater! No, thanks. He's too touchy for me.'

'What's the matter? Did he rebuff you, Rona? Is that the reason for such acrimony in your voice?'

'Don't be silly, Anton.' She was annoyed, perhaps he was too close to the truth in his conjecture. 'Look at those brutes — I adore Alsatians.' She changed the subject, rolling over on to her stomach.

Anton turned over and followed the direction in which she was looking. Kerry could be seen clearly on the cliff top exercising his two dogs.

'Yes, they are handsome brutes,' Anton agreed. 'But lately I've taken a fancy to cats — Siamese cats!' he went on with a twinkle in his eyes. She shot him a scornful look.

'I can't believe that! You aren't the effeminate type. Don't tease, Anton darling. You are strange to-day — what's up?'

He shook his head laughingly. 'Nothing. Don't you like being teased?'

'When I can enjoy the joke — yes. But I feel that you're having a secret laugh at my expense — as though there's something I don't know which amuses you!' She replied with a trace of dejection in her voice. He put his arm around her and hugged her.

'Of course not. Don't be silly. I'm just in the mood to tease you, darling.' He kissed her throat tenderly. Their eyes met, hers full of promise and his of longing. She smiled slowly, tantalizingly and he tightened his grasp on her suddenly so that she drew in her breath sharply

Bill and Ailsa ran after the beach ball in their direction and, having retrieved it, sank down beside Anton and Rona on the sand, puffing and laughing. Olwen and Nadia, after a few moments' vain wait for the couple to return with the ball, came over to join them.

They were a merry party. A couple of hours later, Kerry came down to the beach accompanied by Barry and Jay and carrying a large hamper, the dogs excitedly running on and leaping back to scamper about their feet. The hamper contained a picnic tea which all of them thoroughly enjoyed — especially with the added condiment of Kentish sand. As Anton remarked to

Rona, perhaps the best part of beach picnics was the sand in the sandwiches and the taste of salt in the tea.

Anton hardly gave Ruth a passing thought during the day. If he thought of her at all, it was merely to hope that she was enjoying herself with Gregg. He wondered idly where they were and what they were doing. As for himself, he was thoroughly happy at the moment. He was proving that a man could be married and still enjoy life — and freedom — to the full.

They returned to the house in the early evening, retiring to their rooms to bath and change for dinner. Anton mused idly that one always felt particularly grubby after an afternoon on the beach — but it was pleasant to lie in the sun on the hot sand. Of course, it was early yet. If the bay hadn't been sheltered by the cliff, the cool breeze might have been very disconcerting. He liked July and August, when one could hope for really scorching weather and get as tanned as a berry. He decided that when he left the cast of *A Question of Murder?* he would give himself a brief holiday abroad — the Riviera or Spain, where he could really revel in the sun. Perhaps he would take Rona with him if he was still enjoying her attractions. Ruth could be packed off to her home in Sussex — he was determined that his wife would never intrude into his private life. Anton made the decisions in his marriage and Ruth would very soon realize it, if she hadn't already done so.

★ ★ ★

After dinner, Anton strolled out on to the terrace and stood smoking, watching the sea in the distance. What a wonderful position to have a house, he thought idly, on top of a cliff overlooking the sea, with one's own private bay. One day he would leave the theatre for good and buy himself a nice, sprawling old house in Kent or Sussex.

Of course, he could buy a house now, if he chose, but all his commitments were in town and the mews flat in Mayfair suited him admirably. Ruth seemed happy enough there. She should find something to do — a pity she wasn't talented. If she could occupy her time with paints and palette, or with pen and paper, then he wouldn't have to worry about her when she was alone — he didn't want her to feel neglected, but he really didn't have the time to spend with her. He thought wryly that most married women seemed to waste no time in producing a couple of children and then devoted the rest of their lives to being rather stolid, placid mothers to the brats and unalleviated bores to their friends. Well, he determined, Ruth wasn't going to be condemned to such a life. She was far too young to tie herself down with children and he was far too old to want them around him, so no problem arose. It did not occur to Anton that Ruth might long for a child. Why should she? It was

Anton's experience that the majority of young women went to great lengths to prevent such a catastrophe in their social lives.

Jay Scott followed him on to the terrace and stood for a few moments watching him, before he strolled over to join him. 'Hi there, Anton! Communing with your soul?' he asked satirically. Anton turned to welcome him with a smile.

'Not on your life! I was just envying Kerry this lovely house — and that rather charming little wife of his.' He took out his cigarette case and offered it to Jay, who took one with a nod of thanks. Anton threw away the stub of his cigarette and helped himself to a fresh one, then, flicking his lighter, he lit both cigarettes.

'Nadia? Mm. She is rather sweet. Of course, she won't last,' Jay said authoritatively. 'I grant you that she has something new — an air of candour that is appealing and remarkably novel, but I'm afraid she is already beginning to lose her popularity. Not exciting enough. Now take Jill Ramsay! She certainly has got something. Wait till the *première* of her latest film — I should say her first film. Have you noticed her eyes? They absolutely spell s-e-x! At least they will to the masses.'

'They do to Keith Winter.'

'She's wasting her time there. Silly little fool! I don't know why her studio don't warn her off that unprincipled dago.'

Anton nodded. 'She'll get her fingers burnt. Maybe that's what she wants. But I'm sorry you don't think Nadia will make the grade. I rather admire her.'

'But, man, she can't *act*! How many of them can, these days? Anyway, I don't think it's in the best of taste to malign my hostess's acting abilities, and it isn't what I sought you out for, either. I heard a little bit of gossip the other day which may interest you, Anton.'

'Oh? What was that?'

'A little bird told me that you came out of Caxton Hall about a month ago with a bride on your arm? True or false?' Jay waited for any forthcoming reaction.

Anton laughed. He was not an actor for nothing. If he were taken aback, he didn't show it. Actually, he had known he would have remarks like this one to contend with. It wasn't the first time he had been attributed with secret marriages. 'Who? Rona Grant-Hawkeley again?'

'Not this time. That's the surprising thing. She was an unknown.'

'To me as well, I assure you. You've been well and truly misinformed, old boy!' Anton told the lie steadily. Jay flicked his cigarette into the shrubbery.

'Really? Pity. I thought I was on to a good thing. My informant was very sure.'

'Which just goes to prove that you can't trust any little bird these days, Jay.' Anton grinned at him and Jay shrugged his shoulders.

'I shall have to tell this particular bird to see an oculist,' he murmured and they changed the subject. Anton felt relief. Jay was a wily customer. He knew most things that went on in their circle and there were very few incidents he didn't know of almost before they occurred. After a few moments of conversation, they went into the house.

* * *

When Anton woke the next morning, he felt a stirring of anger against himself, and dark depression descended. For the first few moments of consciousness he had expected to see the sleeping figure of Ruth in her bed next to his. It was odd how quickly he had become used to sharing his bedroom with her — and odd how much he missed her this morning. He thought with nostalgia of the occasions when she had crept in by his side and curled against him, her chin on his shoulder. He suddenly realized that this was the first time he had really missed Ruth.

Now he resented the disturbing effect Rona had on him and hungered for the sweetness of Ruth — modest, unassuming and undemanding Ruth. Women were the very devil! He scowled in his black humour. Rona played havoc with his senses and Ruth played merry hell with his conscience. Why couldn't he forget Ruth when he was on pleasure bent?

He joined the others at breakfast with his mood only partially lightened. Rona was not yet down. Only Jay, Barry and Ailsa were having breakfast. The others had eaten earlier.

''Morning, Anton. You look grim. Perhaps late nights don't suit you,' Barry greeted him. Anton helped himself to bacon and grilled kidneys, coffee and toast and sat down with a wry smile at Barry.

'I should be used to those,' he rejoined. 'If I do look grim, it must be hunger.'

'Hungry? I thought I saw you steal

138

down the corridor in the early hours,' Jay commented dryly. 'I thought you were going to raid the pantry.'

Anton looked at him sharply, but Jay's steely eyes were inscrutable. How much did Jay know or guess? He shrugged — not that he cared a fig for Jay's opinion. 'Good heavens, no! I ceased raiding pantries when I was quite young.'

'Now stolen fruit interests you more, eh?' Jay asked quietly. This time there could be no mistake about his meaning. Anton did not answer, applying himself to the meal.

'Anton, will you make up a four this morning at tennis?' Ailsa broke from her conversation with Barry to ask him.

'Sorry, Ailsa.' He shook his head. 'For one thing, I didn't bring any gear — for another, I don't feel in the mood for anything strenuous this morning.' He smiled his apologies. Rona caught his words as she entered.

'Is this tennis? I'd love a game,' she

139

cried quickly. Ailsa turned to her.

'I thought *you* would. I'm trying to persuade Anton to play. Won't you help me?'

'I haven't much influence with Anton, I'm afraid,' Rona smiled, joining them with a cup of coffee in her hand. She smiled at Anton as she sat down beside him. 'Wouldn't you like to play, darling?' She spoke appealingly, almost persuasively.

'No, I'd rather not. I'm sure you'll find someone else to make up a set — how about you, Jay? You'll make a fine partner for Rona — have you ever seen Jay play, Rona?' He turned to her quickly.

All eyes were on Jay as he shot Anton a dour look. 'Well, Jay?' Rona spoke to him with a warm invitation in her eyes. He smiled at her despite the dourness of his first reaction. He shrugged his shoulders.

'If this is being press-ganged, it's better than I thought,' he retorted. 'Look like that, Rona, and how can I refuse? I'll gladly be your partner.' Rona flashed Anton a triumphant glance. He nodded, agreeing her victory. Jay got to his feet. 'I'll go and change into whites. See you on the court in ten minutes.'

Ailsa rose too. 'We'd better go and put the nets up, Barry. Coming, Rona? 'Bye, Anton.'

Rona waited till the others had left the room, then she leaned nearer to Anton, a meaningly intimate look in her eyes.

'D'you mind being left alone, darling?' she asked, touching his hand with a brief caress. He shook his head.

'Of course not. Go ahead and have fun. I shall probably stroll along the cliff or find Kerry for a game of billiards.'

Rona pouted. 'Not very entertaining. I wish I hadn't agreed to play, now.'

'Don't be silly. You'll enjoy the game. Run along, my dear. I might come along to watch you later.'

She rose a little reluctantly.

'All right. See you later then.' Still

with reluctance, she left the room after dropping a brief kiss on his dark hair.

It was a colder day than the previous one. It was slightly cloudy and in the distance there was a hint of dark storm-clouds.

Anton decided not to leave it too late before returning to London. He knew Rona expected him to drive her home, but he was averse to the idea. It solved itself, however. When he spoke to Rona later that day, she refused his offer to drive her back to London; she refused, smiling, but he fancied that underneath her surface pleasantry she was in fact extremely annoyed with him.

'No, thanks, Anton. I'm staying over until Tuesday. Then I shall probably travel with Jay.'

'Jay? Is he staying over too?'

'Obviously, darling,' she chided him slightly. 'He decided that he would while we were playing tennis.'

'Oh, I see.' Anton thought that for a misogynist, Jay didn't waste his time. 'I meant to ask you before — how did you travel down?'

'You weren't interested before,' she corrected him, 'else you'd have offered me a lift. As a matter of fact, I came with Barry and Ailsa.'

'Darling, don't be illogical. I didn't expect you to wait around for me and then drive down here at dead of night after the show,' he snapped.

'Oh. Well, don't worry about me, Anton. Jay will look after me quite well, I'm sure.' She lifted her head angrily, provocatively.

He pulled her into his arms. 'Not too well!' he told her sharply and kissed her forcefully. She wrenched her head away.

'I shall please myself.' She was annoyed at his possessiveness — a show which was slightly too late, she thought. He had been indifferent to her all the day — not once had he sought her company — he couldn't blame her for finding solace and congenial company elsewhere. Also Jay could be rather attractive when he chose.

Anton released her abruptly. 'All right. Do you think I mind? Good heavens, Rona, you're not the only woman in my life. There are lots of women and one is very much like another.' She paled and he watched her, gratified, glad to see he had hurt her.

'Darling, don't let's quarrel.' She threw herself into his arms. 'Why *are* we quarrelling? You know that Jay is unimportant — he doesn't mean a thing!'

'Then keep it that way,' he retorted grimly and, detaching her arms, walked away. She looked after him, anger ripping through her. How dare he dictate to her? No man had ever told her what to do and Anton Radinov wasn't going to be the first, no matter how much she cared for him. If she chose to have an affair with Jay, then an affair she would have and Anton could jump in the lake.

7

Easter slipped by amazingly quickly for Ruth. She had looked forward to the week-end, for she liked Gregg and enjoyed his company. He had been her escort several times during the last week. They had shopped together, gone to art galleries and museums together, finding several mutual tastes. Anton was glad that Ruth wasn't lonely and that Gregg seemed to admire her enough to seek her out. She was much happier lately, he thought.

Gregg had taken her to dine and dance, to the theatre and the cinema and seemed to devote himself to amusing her, all in good friendship. Ruth found herself growing fonder of him every day, but she adored Anton and always would.

On Easter Sunday, Gregg arrived at the flat very early. Ruth had been up for some time and had breakfast prepared for them both. She had been lonely in the flat on her own, although it was not the first time that Anton had left her to spend the night alone since they were married. She often wondered where he went on such nights, but had never questioned him. They sat over breakfast in high humour, Ruth looking exceptionally pretty and bright-eyed. Gregg knew by now that he was irrevocably in love with her. There was nothing he could do — she obviously was in love with her husband and, Gregg granted, rightly so — therefore his love for her was unavailing, but that could make no difference to his feelings. He saw no reason why he should not devote his time to giving her the fun and laughter and entertainment that Anton apparently forgot about.

Gregg could not help thinking how pleasant it was to sit here with Ruth, sharing breakfast with her. It would be wonderful if he could look forward to a lifetime of such breakfasts with

Ruth, but that was impossible — so he quickly rejected the thought.

He was looking forward to their day out together. She looked fresh and charming in blue linen: her newly washed hair gleamed even brighter in the sunshine and curled riotously over her small, well-shaped head. Gregg thought ironically how much lovelier she was than the majority of women he knew who spent hours in their beauty salons and hairdressers — yet he knew Ruth washed her own hair and used little make-up. Gregg watched her pour coffee delicately, then she handed him his cup with a radiant, affectionate smile that lit up her grey eyes.

Within a couple of hours they were speeding along the dusty main road leading to Ailster, a tiny coastal town of Kent. The breeze ruffled her curls and raised Gregg's bronze hair slightly, even though he had damped it down heavily to discipline the rebellious waves. They sang hit tunes from a recent show as they sped along.

Ruth smiled into Gregg's eyes sunnily, contented and relaxed. Occasionally her thoughts drifted to Anton. She wondered what he was doing, whether he was enjoying his week-end with his friends, what time he had arrived the previous night, and certainly whether he missed her, but Gregg was quick to distract her with merry chatter and laughing banter.

She looked about her happily, eyes shining. She suddenly tucked her hand into Gregg's arm, snuggling close to him. He looked down at her briefly, tenderly, thinking how much he loved her — realizing that nothing but affection had activated the gesture. He sighed, knowing he could never possess her.

It was almost perfect, Ruth thought afterwards, the Easter Sunday she spent with Gregg. If he had been Anton, and as charming and as attentive, Ruth would have wished for nothing more. Whereas Gregg could not forget that although he loved Ruth she was still Anton's wife and as such was unattainable. If she was happy with Anton he did not mind. He was glad that she could find happiness in another man's arms. But Gregg was not so sure that Ruth was happy.

The weather was perfect. The warm, benevolent sun smiled down on them benevolently. The calm waves gently trickled their way up on to the beach and ebbed again just as gently. They had not chosen a desolate spot. They both liked people too much for that. Ailster was not a big coastal town with loads of trippers and charabancs, but a tiny place which welcomed the occasional family party, children with their young parents or nurses; young lovers seeking a warm place in the sun and a few moments of quiet content in each other's company, oblivious to other people; the pair in the sunset of life, who sat hand in hand in their deckchairs, smiling gently and placidly on their fellow-beings, remembering their own youth and happy gaiety on long-ago beaches.

Ruth revelled in the warm sand and the sun. She could scarcely wait until they had finished their picnic lunch, when Gregg allowed her to slip out of her dress, revealing her swimsuit beneath. He had refused to let her lie in the sun in such little clothing earlier, reminding her that it was as yet only April and that the day wasn't warm enough before lunch. They swam, frolicked on the beach with a ball, then lay talking in the sun, quite contented, munching sandwiches and drinking flask tea.

Gregg had always preferred the simple things in life, but he had never enjoyed them so much as on this outing with Ruth. The day went all too quickly. Gregg made Ruth slip into her dress as the sun seemed to lose some of its warmth towards the end of the afternoon. Pouting, she did so. 'I'm quite warm still,' she protested, nonetheless obeying him.

'You may catch a chill and I won't

take the responsibility. Anton would never forgive me if I didn't look after you properly,' Gregg told her, helping her on with a cardigan.

'I sometimes wonder if he'd care,' she muttered almost under her breath, but Gregg caught the bitter words. 'Anyway,' she went on, more brightly, 'I'm old enough to look after myself.'

'I don't dispute that,' he returned, choosing to ignore her first remark. 'But surely you wouldn't deny me the pleasure of looking after you.' She gave him a quick, warm smile.

'All right, Sir Lancelot. I surrender.'

'That's a good girl!' he commended her, giving her a quick hug. She flung her arms around him impulsively, returning his embrace.

'You're fun, Gregg. I wish Anton were more like you,' she said suddenly. Gregg's eyes clouded.

'I often wish I were Anton,' he returned slowly, with deep yearning. She looked at him swiftly. Their eyes met and she frowned, an anxious look clouding her face.

'Gregg, please don't grow too fond of me.' He did not answer her. 'I don't want you to be hurt,' she went on. 'Remember, I'm married to Anton.'

'D'you think its possible for me to forget that?' he countered swiftly, bitterly. Then, sensing that she was troubled: 'You're very conceited if you think I'm falling for you, my girl. You shouldn't jump to conclusions — certainly not without any encouragement.' She smiled a little doubtfully. 'Don't worry, Ruth,' he said urgently and put his hand under her chin to raise her face, smiling into her eyes. She could not resist smiling back at him. He jumped up and pulled her to her feet. 'Come on! Let's drive round the neighbouring countryside, find a nice ancient pub and have a good old-fashioned country tea. I could eat a horse. How does that appeal?'

'The country tea or the horse?' she teased, and they laughed together. Ruth danced ahead towards the car, Gregg close on her heels, carrying the hamper basket and the rugs.

That evening, when Gregg had left her at the flat with a promise to call early the next day, as they were going to the London Zoo, Ruth was a little worried about the incident. But slipping into bed she put the worry aside. Gregg was too sensible to let himself care too much for a married woman, she assured herself.

Monday was not so warm as the previous day and Ruth was glad of her short jacket over the summer dress she wore. Her hands thrust in her pockets, she sauntered beside Gregg, not oblivious to the admiration he drew from several women they passed. She felt pleased to be with him. He was so tall and striking and although no one could call Gregg handsome, she thought idly, his features being too irregular, he was very attractive with his oddly crooked smile and blue eyes.

The Zoo was crowded; always a popular place, it seemed to Ruth and

Gregg that the world and his wife were there that day. Ruth loved animals and Gregg delighted in watching her sunny face light up with pleasure at sight of the small deer, the penguins, the baby polar bears who had been born that spring and were on show for the first time, the long-necked giraffe with her ungainly, long-legged, pathetic baby. It seemed to be the small and helpless animals that appealed most to Ruth. He looked down at her, smiling with tenderness. Feeling his glance, she looked quickly at him, but he drew her attention to the antics of a penguin as he waddled his way down to the water's edge, enchanting and immaculate in his black tails and boiled shirt-front!

They lunched in one of the Zoo restaurants and then found a well-kept lawn where they could sit for a while and smoke a cigarette leisurely. Gregg sat with his knees drawn up to his chin, chewing a piece of grass thoughtfully, while Ruth watched the passing people, playing idly with the grass.

She always felt a keen interest in other people and loved to study them. Wives and husbands with their young children, young girls in groups, men and their girl-friends, elderly couples walking at a slow pace; harassed mothers trying to control wandering babies and growing children, who were mischievous and naughty in their childish ways. The day was growing warmer as the afternoon wore on and Ruth slipped out of her coat. They did not talk much. Ruth was intent on the people who passed by, Gregg was busy with his thoughts.

Suddenly Gregg stiffened, catching sight of Les Power and Avrina Marsh, the latter beautifully elegant as always, picking her way across the grass towards them in high heels.

'Here's Avrina Marsh with Les Power. D'you know them?' Gregg turned to Ruth. 'Avrina is Anton's co-star at the moment.'

'I know Les. And of course I've seen

Miss Marsh at the theatre. She's lovely, isn't she?'

'Hello, Gregg!' Les greeted them as he and his companion reached them. 'Avrina was so sure it was you when we were at the top of Bear Walk that she insisted on coming to make sure. She said she couldn't mistake that flaming mop of yours and she was right.' Les threw himself to the grass beside them. Avrina sank down gracefully with a gracious smile which included both Gregg and Ruth.

'What are you two doing here? I shouldn't have thought the Zoo was your *métier*,' Gregg teased. 'By the way, Les, you know Ruth — David Harmer's cousin.' Les nodded, smiling at Ruth. 'Avrina?' Gregg turned to the lovely actress.

'We haven't met before. How d'you do?' She nodded to Ruth almost disinterestedly, then without waiting for Ruth's answer turned to Gregg. 'My dear, I absolutely adore the Zoo. I love animals.'

'So do I!' exclaimed Ruth quickly. Avrina smiled at her with a little more warmth.

'It must be a change to stare at the animals, Avrina — a change from having animals stare at you, I mean, darling,' Gregg said laughingly. Avrina nodded.

'It is a relief. I come here to get rid of all my repressions, making fun of the amusing little animals behind bars. Its so nice to be out of the limelight for once.'

She spoke sincerely enough, yet Ruth had the fleeting impression that being out of the limelight did not suit Avrina Marsh at all. Also she felt a certain resentment at the implication of mockery in Avrina's remark. She fell silent, a little shy and slightly overawed by this elegant and self-confident woman. Ruth sat listening to the three exchanging pleasantries. After a few moments, Avrina turned to speak to her, smiling. 'How *is* David?'

'Oh, I haven't seen him for some

time,' Ruth replied truthfully. 'We don't see much of each other, I'm afraid.'

'Weren't you at the theatre one night with David and Les — wasn't Rona Grant-Hawkeley with you?'

'Oh, yes,' Ruth admitted. 'But that was one of the rare occasions when I see David. He rang me, asking me to make up the theatre party. He does that occasionally. I was thrilled with the play,' she added a little shyly. 'I thought your acting was magnificent.'

'How nice of you to say so. So many people forget that Anton Radinov isn't the only one in the cast — not that I'm jealous, I assure you. I'm the first one to admit how marvellous Anton is.'

Ruth felt a rush of pride at this praise for her husband, then she realized that Avrina had no idea that she was talking to Anton's wife. She coloured when she thought how nearly she had given herself away. 'I thought he was wonderful, too,' she said quietly and was glad that Gregg came to her rescue with a different subject.

'Where's Anton this week-end?' Avrina asked of Gregg some minutes later.

He shrugged. 'Staying with Kerry Moore, I think. He didn't say much to me about his movements.'

'Kerry's married again at last, I see,' Avrina went on. 'That sweet young thing — what *is* her name?'

'Nadia Norris,' supplied Les. 'Enchanting. I met her the other week at a cocktail party. She was with Kerry. They seem ideally suited.'

'Really?' Avrina's tone was slightly acid. 'I can't imagine Kerry falling for a simpering little starlet. Not at his age! I wonder how long she will last — what is she, his fourth wife?'

'Oh, come now, Avrina,' protested Gregg. 'Only his third. Don't be feminine. You shouldn't advertise your unrequited love, darling.'

'My dear Gregg, don't be ridiculous. I'm very fond of Kerry, of course — we've known each longer than

159

I care to remember — but as for love . . . ' she laughed. 'Actually, I had my chance some time ago. He asked me to marry him. I refused.'

'You refused!' Gregg exclaimed in mock astonishment. 'How could you deny yourself the opportunity of being Mrs. Kerry Moore? Perhaps you hate being just one of a crowd?'

'It was more a question of not denying Kerry his third adventure into matrimony with a fascinating and brainless child. He was obviously attracted to Nadia at the time of his proposal to me, but felt that we had known each other so long that it was time he made our association legal. Naturally, I refused.'

'Quite understandable.' Gregg nodded, but his blue eyes twinkled with laughter.

'Is Rona going to be at Kerry's place this week-end?' asked Les suddenly. 'I'm sure she said she was.'

'I wouldn't be surprised!' cut in Avrina with a meaning laugh. Gregg frowned. The subject was on dangerous ground he knew.

'It's possible,' he replied. 'I understand it's quite a large house-party.'

'Rona had a handsome man — his love was all aglow, everywhere that Rona went — Don Juan was sure to go!' chanted Avrina maliciously, a feminine gleam in her eye.

Ruth listened, failing at first to see the connection. Then she remembered that Anton's nickname in the gossip columns was Don Juan! She went cold with sudden, nameless fear.

'Yes,' went on Les, 'Anton's still amazingly wrapped up in Rona. I had no idea the affair would last so long. She must have something the others lacked!'

'Or else she's more willing to part with what she *has* got!' Avrina laughed maliciously. 'Which is more like it, with a man like Anton Radinov. Thank goodness he's never cut any ice with me. I should hate to be one of a crowd!'

'Aren't you being a little unfair?' Gregg broke in. 'Slandering Anton is neither just nor wise. You know you love to gossip, Avrina — there's no truth in any of the things you're saying.'

Ruth could listen no longer. She, too, could imagine and felt sudden revulsion.

'Gregg — I don't feel well. Would you take me home?' She stood up. In all truth she did not look well, as she swayed slightly, the whiteness of her cheeks alarming, her eyes dangerously bright. Gregg leapt to his feet.

'Of course, Ruth.'

Les looked up at her. 'You certainly look very pale. Too much sun?'

'Probably.' Ruth tried to smile at him. He grinned back, a pleasant-faced young man who was usually lost in thought, designing his latest scenery, while conversation flowed around him.

'Have a good time, you two!' Gregg said to Avrina and Les. 'Take my advice and leave the slander alone.'

162

He smiled to relieve his words of the sting. Avrina's only reply was a mocking laugh.

★ ★ ★

When they reached the flat, Ruth was still pale and yet strangely calm. Gregg had half expected that she would dissolve into tears as soon as they reached the sanctuary of the car although he knew it was not her nature to show her emotions unduly. She had stared straight ahead during the journey, silent, her hands clasped tightly in her lap.

'Please — don't come in with me,' she said quietly as he pulled up outside the mews. 'I want to be alone for a while. I've had a lovely day, Gregg. But I think I have had too much sun — my head aches badly,' she lied.

'You don't have to lie to me, Ruth,' he said gently. 'Darling, please don't think twice about Avrina's remarks. She's a jealous woman and therefore rather malicious. I swear to you that she wasn't speaking the truth.' She didn't even notice the endearment and his words fell on hard ground.

'Don't bother to defend Anton,' she answered stonily. She was remembering the nights that Anton had spent away from the flat, days when he had gone out in bad temper and stayed out: also days when he had been oddly over-affectionate towards her, as though showing remorse for something he had done that she knew nothing about. Now she felt it was all clear to her. 'I don't for one moment believe that Anton is capable of disloyalty to me.' But for the time being she did.

Gregg watched her as she walked over the cobblestones to the side door which led to the flat. His eyes were troubled. He wanted desperately to follow her, to take her in his arms and comfort her, to protect her from all hurt and pain. He cursed Anton savagely, then drove off.

8

Anton arrived home just after seven o'clock.

Ruth was seated in the window-seat, reading a magazine. At least the book was in her hands, and occasionally she remembered to turn a page, but she was unaware of the words. She found her mind too confused to read.

She knew Anton's life before he married her had involved several love affairs, but she could not believe that he would continue to parade a mistress since his marriage. But facts seemed to point to this. He had been eager to spend the weekend away from Ruth, refusing to cancel his arrangements. Probably Rona was waiting for him with loving arms, and he had been impatient for her embrace.

Didn't he care that he humiliated Ruth in the eyes of so many, she asked herself despairingly.

As she heard Anton's key in the lock, her heart leapt; she determined to greet him as she always did, but it had occured to her to confront him with the gossip and discover his reaction. She dismissed this idea. What if it were lies and she accused him of adultery! He would possibly be angry enough to walk out — decide to end their marriage if it appeared that his wife thought so little of his character and placed so little trust in him.

He strode in, tossing his gloves and coat down on the chair in his familiar way. Ruth usually ran to pick them up and put them away in a wifely manner, but to-night his action pained her. She visualized him doing the same thing at Rona's flat, and Rona hurrying to put them away with a great show of loving tolerance.

'Hello, Ruth.' He came over and bent to kiss her hair. He thought suddenly that he had missed her more than he realized at the time. She raised her head and smiled, a little hesitantly. Anton wondered why she seemed so forlorn. 'Did Gregg look after you?'

'Yes, thank you, Anton.' Her reply was quiet and a little cold. She put the magazine aside and watched him as he strode to the cabinet to pour himself a drink.

'He's a reliable chap,' he said absent-mindedly.

'Did you have a good time?' she asked slowly.

He paused before answering to drain the whisky in his glass. Then he nodded.

'Wonderful! I enjoyed the break — and they're a good crowd.' He yawned suddenly. 'I feel tired, though. It was a hectic week-end.'

'Who was there? Anyone I know?' She forced her voice to appear casual.

'I don't know, really. Kerry, of course, and Nadia, his wife. Barry Preston and his wife, Ailsa. Two film starlets — Jill Ramsay and Olwen Evans. Ah, by the way, Jay was there.

You know Jay Scott?' Ruth nodded in answer to his enquiring glance. 'A few others,' he went on. 'Quite a merry crowd.'

He made no mention of Rona, and a knife twisted in Ruth's breast. Anton was surprised at her silence. Usually when he came in she was pleased to see him, and chattered away to him happily. 'Is anything wrong, Ruth?'

She shook her head and tried to speak lightly. 'No. Only a headache. I think I was out in the sun too long . . . ' Her voice trailed off.

'Poor darling.' He flung himself down into an easy chair and held out his hand to her. 'Come here, my sweet, and tell me about your week-end.' She slowly got to her feet and went over to him. Slipping his arm about her, he drew her on to his knee. 'It's nice to see you, Ruth,' he said sincerely.

'Is it?'

'Mm. Now tell me. What did you and Gregg do?' He put his head back against the chair and waited for her answer.

Ruth hesitated. Then she shrugged her shoulders slightly. 'Nothing very important. We went to Ailster, in Kent, on Sunday. It's a lovely little place, and we had a laze in the sun and a swim, then went on for tea at a pub.'

'Sounds pleasant,' Anton commented.

'It was. Then to-day we went to the Zoo at Regent's Park.'

'Not very exciting.'

'Oh, it was.' Ruth thought that he couldn't know how disturbing a visit it had been.

'Good. Well, I'm glad you enjoyed yourself.' He looked at her a little more closely. 'You are rather pale, darling. Don't you think it would do you good to go to bed?'

'It's much too early,' she protested.

'Is it?' He glanced at his watch. 'Yes, I suppose it is. Well, look, Ruth, I have to go out' — then as he saw her eyes darken — 'yes, I know, it's beastly, but I promised to drop in on

169

Sol for a drink to-night. He's having a party and I can't let him down. You don't mind, do you?' He spoke almost pleadingly, and ran his hand over her hair.

She signed gently. 'No, I don't mind, Anton.'

When he had gone, she felt depression creep over her gently, and she knew that tears pricked her eyelids.

She had a bath and took time over it, letting the warm, scented water refresh her body and ease her spirit. Then she made herself some tea and took the tray into the bedroom. She was glad to slip between the cool sheets. She left her tea untouched; lying in the darkness, trying to find an answer to Anton's behaviour, tears were near the surface.

When Anton came home, some little while later, but not as late as she had expected, he was very careful not to disturb Ruth, thinking her asleep. He undressed in the lounge, slipping into his dressing-robe, and entered the bedroom without switching on the lights. He walked quietly to the side of her bed and leaned over his wife.

'I'm awake, Anton,' she said quietly, her heart pounding with the fear that he meant to kiss her. She could not have suffered the touch of his lips — lips that she was sure had been kissing Rona such a short time ago.

He was startled. 'I thought you were asleep. I've been so careful not to waken you,' he said, switching on the lamp.

'I know. I couldn't sleep.'

'Does your head still ache?' he asked tenderly. Sitting on her bed, he drew her into his arms and stroked her hair with a caressing, gentle movement. She lay passive. 'Is that better?' he asked after a few moments. Then, as she nodded: 'Good. Pleased to have me home, Ruth?'

'Of course,' she said evasively. 'I missed you.' While you dallied with your red-headed mistress, her heart cried in anger and pain.

'I missed you, too.' He pressed his lips to her hair, his arms tightening about her. Liar — liar, her heart cried. She struggled in his arms, recognizing awakening passion in his hold.

'Anton — I'm tired,' she said quickly, drawing away from him. His eyes filled with disappointment, but he made no protest. She regretted her words as soon as he stood up. She longed for his arms about her, his lips hard on hers. With passion, perhaps, he could deaden the ache in her heart, the thoughts in her brain. But too proud to call his name, she turned away from him, over on to her side, and pulled her covers high around her neck. He stood looking down at her, puzzled. Then, a little angry and disappointed, he got into his own bed and switched off the light.

Ruth lay tense. Though she had refused him, now she longed for his embrace. Pain caught at her heart. It seemed hours before she finally slept.

★ ★ ★

During the days that followed, Anton was busy making arrangements to leave his present production, busy with plans for the next play. He was also planning a brief holiday in Spain, and hardly noticed Ruth's preoccupation and coldness towards him.

Ruth was most unhappy. She found that she was watching for any little slip that Anton might make. She constantly worried if Rona were his mistress, and if so, why? The newspapers did not help. One morning, picking up a daily paper, she found a fresh story about her husband and Rona. They had been seen in a night club, and the paper carried an intimate photograph, their heads close together in a dimly lit corner. The accompanying article rumoured an engagement, born of an overheard remark. Ruth was filled with anger. On the point of informing the newspaper that she was Anton's wife, and therefore he was not in a position to become engaged to anyone, she paused with her hand on the instrument. What was the use? It would only make Anton angry and, at the moment, Ruth had no wish for the world to know that, married to one woman, he was capable of an affair with another. It would be too humiliating, she thought, shuddering at the imagined newspaper stories.

When Anton was home, Ruth deliberately found things to do which kept her from keeping him company. He usually went out in the evenings and by the time he returned Ruth was in bed and asleep. If he noticed how aloof she was, he gave no sign of it. But one day, wondering perhaps if he had neglected her a little of late, he brought her home a present. For a few moments Ruth forgot her unhappiness and quickly opened the small parcel, her eyes shining. A smile lit her face for the first time in days. She drew out a diamond bracelet and stared at it, speechless. It was the first time she had ever owned diamonds, certainly never anything so lovely. She gazed at it wide-eyed, held it against her wrist, then to her cheek, then leapt up to fly into his arms.

Anton held her close, smiling. 'I'm glad you like it, Ruth.'

A sudden thought struck her as she met his eyes and she drew away, horrified. With pale cheeks and pain-darkened eyes, she replaced the bracelet in its protective coverings. 'What is it? A peace-offering?' she asked, with bitterness in her voice.

'A peace-offering? What do you mean? I don't understand you . . . '

'Don't you?' she interrupted. She turned to face him, breast heaving, eyes blazing. 'Don't you? Can you deny that you had a motive for buying me such an expensive gift?'

'But — of course there is. I wanted to give you a present — you've been so unapproachable lately. I thought I'd upset you somehow. Perhaps it is a peace-offering in that sense. But does a man need a motive to give his wife . . . '

'Annoyed me? A mild way of

putting it,' she snapped. He frowned and moved to take her back into his arms.

'Ruth, what have I done? I can't remember upsetting you, but if I did . . .'

'Don't touch me,' she cried, evading his embrace. 'You're despicable — don't touch me!'

He shrugged, dropping his arms. 'Very well. But I shall be grateful if you'll tell me what I'm supposed to have done.'

'No!' She ran into the kitchen and slammed the door. With rising annoyance Anton threw himself into an armchair and lit his pipe, scowling. He glared at the bracelet which lay where Ruth had left it — so much for his good intentions. She was so strange, almost indifferent to him lately. It was unlike her to show temper, not to mention other little things about her behaviour of late that he had seen but not really noticed before.

When Anton went to bed that night

he sat down beside Ruth and put a tentative hand on her shoulder. Since her outraged behaviour over the bracelet she had not spoken to him, ignoring him completely. Finally he had left the flat and sought Rona's company. Greeting him very warmly, she had soon soothed his injured pride.

Ruth stiffened under his touch. How dare he? No doubt he had come straight from Rona!

'Ruth!' He spoke her name gently. She made no reply. 'Are you asleep?' he asked. Getting no answer, he brushed back a stray lock of hair with a tender, almost loving touch. There was a gentleness in the gesture which pricked Ruth's eyes with unshed tears. But pride held her back. Her lashes nevertheless fluttered and Anton realized that she was awake. 'Come on, I know you're not sleeping,' he said quickly. 'Sit up, Ruth, I want to talk to you.' Defeated, she sat up, brushing her hair back and glancing pointedly at the clock.

'You've picked a fine time for talking,' she told him coldly.

'That doesn't matter. Now look here, let's get a few things straight. You've been treating me like a leper ever since I spent that week-end away from you at Easter. Why?'

'Do you mean to tell me that you've really noticed?' Ruth's voice was heavy with sarcasm.

'Don't be sarcastic. Really, Ruth, you've changed completely lately. What happened to the sweet girl I married?'

'Was I sweet when we were married?' she asked cynically.

'I happened to think so,' he told her quietly and she felt a sudden rush of shame. 'Ruth, tell me what's wrong?'

'Nothing. It's your imagination,' she replied.

'My imagination isn't that colourful,' he retorted. 'I'm sick of your evasion, Ruth. Why are you so cold towards me?'

'Am I?' She looked at him with an

innocent stare; she was deliberately being aggravating and it annoyed him.

'For God's sake, Ruth!' he shouted. 'Stop being so childish and answer me!'

'Don't shout at me!' Ruth was not without spirit.

'I'll shout at you if I please. How else can I get some sense out of you, you damn little fool!' He was very angry now. He took her by the shoulders and shook her. She wrenched herself away furiously, her colour high.

'Take your hands off me. Go and manhandle your mistress — she might appreciate it more!'

Anton stared at her, taken aback. What had possessed her? What did she mean? Had Gregg been filling her head with gossip? How else could she have found out about Rona? Was Gregg trying to break up their marriage with filthy scandal and lies? Anton looked at Ruth for one long moment. Then: 'Darling!' he said gently. The tender endearment caused her to look at him in surprise. It was so unexpected. He put his arms around her with a sudden gesture. She stiffened, but he held her close, stroking her hair. 'So you're angry with me, Ruth. Angry because you've been told a lot of lies?'

'I'm not *angry* with you,' she said sadly, her voice a little muffled. He shook his head.

'Do stop lying, Ruth,' he told her reproachfully.

'But I'm not. It isn't anger I feel — it's disappointment. I thought you were so wonderful.' She began to sob against his shoulder.

'Oh, darling!' he exclaimed in contrition. He let her cry, soothing her gently, caressing her head. 'You know I'm not perfect. I can't deny that I've had affairs with women — before we married. I'm no saint. What did you expect?'

'I didn't expect you to carry on in the same way once we were married,' she cried.

He looked pained. 'What proof have

180

you that I've been carrying on in the same way?'

'None,' she admitted slowly, 'except what I've been told and have heard from other people.'

'Gregg — for instance?'

Her tears were forgotten instantly. Even in his anger, as she looked up at him quickly, he noticed how lovely she managed to look with tears on her lashes and smudges on her cheeks, her hair ruffled and falling about her face.

'It wasn't Gregg! He would never say a word against you — you should know that. He's far too kind and good!'

'I had no idea you held a brief for him. It would seem that he hasn't been wasting his time while I've been busy elsewhere.' Anton felt a sudden resentment against Gregg.

'How can you talk like that of a man who is one of your truest and most loyal friends?' she cried. Her eyes blazed with such contemptuous anger that he knew his accusation to be unfounded. He shrugged his shoulders.

'I'll tell you,' she went on. 'It wasn't Gregg. It was your so-called friends, Les Power and Avrina Marsh. We met them at the Zoo on Easter Monday. They were talking of you and Rona. They didn't know — how could they? — that I was your wife. That's what comes of your stupid secrecy. You were too worried about your publicity! Afraid you'd lose your adoring fans if they discovered you were married. I wish I'd never married you . . . ' She could not stop the flow of bitter words, but the last was completely untrue and, realizing it, she trailed off into a miserable silence. She looked at him timidly. His eyes were suddenly cold and hard, his expression grim.

'I'm sorry about that. But I warned you that you might regret it.' He stood up. ''Still, you won't have to put up with me any longer. I'm going to Spain at the end of the month.'

'Anton!' she cried involuntarily. 'Without me?'

'I shouldn't think that will worry

you. My original intention was to take you, but I wouldn't force my company on you. While I'm gone you can make other arrangements for your life.'

'You can't mean that . . . ' She stared at him, the pain in her heart so intense she almost felt faint.

'Yes, I do. If you find me intolerable to live with, well — it can be remedied. Take the necessary steps. Divorce me. Rona and I will give you the required evidence at any time. Good night, Ruth.'

He turned away. He climbed into his own bed, lay down on his side away from her and pulled the covers up to his chin.

'Anton!' She called his name in anguish. 'Oh, darling!' But he ignored her. He felt miserable and lonely and hurt, but his pride refused to let him accept her peace-offering. Now that Ruth had admitted how much she regretted marrying him, Anton realized that he loved her as deeply as he had never once thought possible. His arms ached to hold her and his spirit was low as he lay, wakeful, thinking of her and how precious she was to him.

The next morning Ruth rose, dressed and prepared Anton's breakfast. When she went in with his tray, he lay curled up on his side in his usual position, head tucked almost out of sight, his dark hair rumpled. Her heart smote her as she looked down on his defenceless features in their repose. She was fearful that he meant to carry out his threat to go to Spain alone, expecting her to divorce him eventually. She longed to throw her arms about him, tell him how dearly she loved him — that she had never really regretted marrying him. No matter how many affairs he might have with other women, Ruth loved him enough to forgive and forget, as long as he always came back to her.

When she called his name gently he opened his eyes. Startled into wakefulness, as always, he sat up quickly. Then as he looked at Ruth he remembered the events of the previous night and his eyes darkened. She offered him the tray, but he brushed her aside, throwing back his covers.

'I don't want anything to eat.'

'Oh, Anton, do have some breakfast,' she pleaded, but he shook his head, pulling on his dressing-gown.

'No, thanks.' He went into the lounge and crossed to the telephone, still nursing his hurt pride. Ruth followed him with the loaded tray in her hands. He shot her a dour glance. 'And stop following me about — I've told you, I don't want anything to eat!' She made no reply, putting down the tray. He picked up the telephone receiver.

'Anton!' she said gently. He looked at her coldly, preparing to dial. Her heart sank as she met the iciness of his glance. 'Can't we forget — I'm sorry about last night . . . oh, Anton darling,' she blurted.

'Can *you* forget?' he asked her bluntly. 'I'm not quite a fool. I know damn well you'll never forget that I went to bed with another woman — and as for forgiving, that's equally out of the question for you. It's obvious that we made a mistake ever to marry. You said as much last night. So we'll disentangle ourselves as neatly and quickly as possible. What else is there to do?'

'We could try again, Anton,' she said hesitantly, and he gave a bitter laugh.

'On what foundation? It was unsafe enough when we married — can't you imagine what it must be like now? Crumbling under our feet! No, Ruth, the whole thing's a washout. You can see my lawyer about a divorce — he's a good man. I'm leaving by plane for Castilio at the end of the month — until I leave, I'll go to a hotel.'

'Why should you leave your flat?' Ruth returned proudly, although she was very near to tears. 'I'll go to a hotel.'

'No, you won't. I don't propose to argue with you.' He dialled a number, indicating that the discussion was closed. Ruth listened while he made arrangements with an hotel for a suite of rooms, her heart twisting inside her body with such intensity that she felt there could be no worse pain in life. As he replaced the receiver, she turned away. He went into the bedroom to dress, then pack. He, too, felt as though his heart was being wrenched from his body, but he firmly believed what he had told Ruth. If they did try again to make a success of their marriage, they had nothing on which to build. If it had foundered after such a short time, obviously it had been a wrong idea in the first place.

Ruth left him alone. She was afraid to meet his eyes again or have him speak to her in that harsh, dry voice, for she knew that the tears would well up and overflow. She had heard that men had no time for crying women and Anton was angry enough already.

Oh, God! she prayed, please let everything be all right. Please let Anton change his mind and come back to me. I love him so much. She laid her head against the window-pane, looking out but seeing nothing.

Anton came into the room a few minutes later, fully dressed, carrying a grip which he put down by the door. He came over and stood by Ruth.

'I'm going now. I'll send for the remainder of my things later. I have enough for the time being.'

'Yes, all right, Anton.' The words choked her, but she fought back the burning, bitter tears.

'I'll be at the Hôtel Villiers if you want me for anything. This is my lawyer's card . . . ' He handed her a small piece of pasteboard which she looked at blindly. 'Do as I said. I'll let you know when I leave for Spain.'

'Is — is Rona going with you?' she asked, unable to hold back the question which was searing her mind.

'No,' he replied curtly. 'But you'll have plenty of evidence without that.'

'Then you admit that she is your — mistress?'

He shrugged. 'I have no choice but

to admit it. You've really forced a confession from me, haven't you?'

She felt a sudden pang of guilt. 'Don't put me in the wrong, Anton!' she cried quickly.

He turned away. 'I'll get in touch with Gantry,' he said. 'Leave everything to him.' He paused, anguish flooding through him. 'I'm sorry it had to be like this, Ruth . . . '

If he had taken her in his arms at that moment all the ensuing unhappiness would have been avoided. But he hesitated — and she ran from the room.

With an unhappy look after her, he picked up his grip and left.

9

Ruth had never been so desperately unhappy. Missing Anton was like an aching void in her heart. The next day she stumbled across his pipe — his favourite pipe — lying forgotten in a corner of the room where it must have rolled. The reminder of him had brought bitter tears.

Days were so long and empty without him — although she had not spent a lot of time with him during the few weeks that their marriage had lasted, at least she had known he would be home at night. She had spent sleepless nights and finally took to drugging herself into oblivion with aspirin: even so, she dreamt frequently of him and woke up sobbing.

For the first few days Ruth felt that she had nothing left in life to live for. Gregg, who was rehearsing for a new play, did not visit her. The flat was a constant reminder of Anton. Yasmin, the kitten, mewed plaintively for Anton: this tore Ruth's heart and she shed many tears on Yasmin's coat.

Gradually, as day succeeded day, Ruth began to think that perhaps Anton would change his mind and come back. Perhaps one day she would hear the familiar sound of his key in the lock and he would come in, take her in his arms and ask her forgiveness. Or no! There would be no need for words. Anton would know that she forgave him and welcomed him back.

Gregg came to see her the following week-end. When she heard the ring of the door-bell, Ruth ran quickly to answer it. Anton? Her heart pounded tumultuously.

Gregg looked down at her, remembering another time when he had called and she had opened the door with that same expectancy in her eyes; he felt a strong surge of love. Hope drained from her face as she realized it was Gregg and not her husband. She stood aside for him to enter.

'Hallo, Ruth. How are you? Sorry I've been neglecting you, but I really have been busy with rehearsals — the script has been changed four times already! We're all going quite mad.'

'Nice to see you, Gregg,' she said dully. He looked at her sharply.

'What's wrong, Ruth? Can I help you?'

'No. No one can help. Anton's gone.' She could not cry. She did not even feel tears rising behind her lids. Too many tears had been shed for Anton and now she was numb.

'Gone? Gone where? What d'you mean, Ruth?' But almost before he asked the question, Gregg knew the answer. 'You poor child!' He took her into his arms with one swift movement and held her close. 'You mean, you've had a bustup. He's walked out on you?'

She nodded, glad of his presence and the comfort of his arms.

'Why? Did you have a showdown — about Rona, perhaps?'

'Yes,' she admitted unhappily.

'He'll be back, Ruth. Don't worry, my dear. I know Anton's tantrums. He'll come back, most repentant and full of promises, I assure you. When did he go?'

'Last Monday. But he won't come back. He wants me to divorce him,' she said, releasing herself. 'Can I have a cigarette, Gregg?'

Wordlessly, he offered his case. Taking one, she lit it from the table-lighter and inhaled deeply.

She expelled the smoke with a little sigh. 'I can only think he wants to marry Rona. Anyway, he told me to start proceedings for divorce.'

'He can't mean that, Ruth.'

'Yes, he does.' Her voice was quite expressionless. 'He made himself quite clear. He's at the Hôtel Villiers — he leaves for Spain next week. I'm to institute proceedings as soon as possible. Oh, Gregg, what am I to do?' Her voice broke slightly.

'There doesn't seem to be anything, except what he asks — divorce him.' Gregg was sorry for the girl: she was so obviously unhappy. But he was not surprised that the marriage was coming to a sticky end. Once she had divorced Anton, in time she might consider marrying again. He loved her and his only wish was for her happiness. In time, Ruth might come to love him — she needed to get this fascination for Anton completely out of her system.

'Anton is a very determined man, Ruth,' he went on. 'If he's made up his mind that your marriage is a failure, nothing on this earth will persuade him that it isn't.'

'So it seems. He hasn't given either of us much chance to make a success of it!' She sounded bitter.

Fond though she was of Gregg, Ruth was relieved when he finally had to leave, reluctant as he was to go. For once, he was no real comfort to her — Ruth felt that he was almost eager for her to divorce Anton. It was the last thing she wanted — while they were still married, Anton might feel the need of her again, might decide to pick up the threads and give marriage another trial. Divorce was so final — so Ruth clung to the frail hope that he would change his mind.

★ ★ ★

Anton made arrangements with his lawyer for a certain sum of money to be at his wife's disposal and Mark Gantry rang Ruth during the week to inform her of Anton's wishes and to invite her to his office to discuss matters.

When she arrived, he greeted her warmly. He was not only Anton's lawyer, but also a personal friend. He had been surprised to discover that Anton was married, and astonished when his friend told him how brief the union had been.

Mark had thought it possible that Anton's wife was simply a gold-digger who had married him for his money and his name, and now sought a tidy income without the inconvenience of a husband about the house. But as she came in, a little shyly, pale and obviously distressed, his thoughts underwent a rapid change. It looked as if the girl was in love with her husband. Pity they hadn't made the marriage work, but that happened so often these days, especially when people married on very slim foundations. Anton had told Mark that he and Ruth had known each other a bare two months when they married — he had heard that cry so often!

Ruth knew very little about divorce or any legal proceedings and she was surprised when Mark told her that there would be a wait of three years before proceedings could be instituted. Also, she felt relief. Three years was a long time and anything could happen. Anton might easily realize that he had been happier living with Ruth than without her.

'Of course,' Mark told her, 'I expect that things could be speeded up if you would like me to see what can be done.'

'I'm in no hurry to divorce my husband, Mr. Gantry. It was never my idea, but Anton so obviously wants to be free that I can only comply.'

'It's a pity that more husbands and wives who are unhappily married and refuse to free their partner, don't think like you, Mrs. Radinov.' He smiled. 'Still, you leave things in my hands. As I said, not much can be done at present. Anton has made complete arrangements for your welfare, you'll want for nothing, he has also signed over the lease of the flat to you and he has paid a year's rental in advance.'

'He has been very kind,' Ruth murmured. 'And so have you. Thank you very much for explaining everything to me.' She rose, smoothing her gloves a little nervously. 'Please believe that all this is repugnant to me. The idea of divorcing Anton is really so horrible that

I'm glad nothing can be done yet. But I wouldn't hold him against his will.'

Mark rose and offered his hand. 'Well, Mrs. Radinov, Anton and I have been friends for years. I've told him so often to marry and settle down — now he's chosen such a charming wife, I very much regret that he feels it was a mistake. I sincerely hope that these proceedings never have to go forward.' They shook hands and Ruth left.

She did not feel at all well. Hurriedly, she summoned a taxi and gave him the address. She could not understand why she felt so faint. Possibly the general unhappiness she felt, the fact that she was neither sleeping nor eating well lately, had a lot to do with the sudden feeling of inertia and giddiness.

★ ★ ★

Anton, settled in his suite at the Hôtel Villiers, certainly felt no happier than his wife. But if he felt a strong desire to seek Ruth and beg her to try again to make a success of their marriage, he pushed the desire aside. What was the use? Ruth obviously hadn't been happy — hadn't she said herself that she regretted marrying him — and all he wanted was her happiness.

He busied himself with final plans for Spain. He looked forward to seeing Castilio again, a place of historic interest. Hot countries appealed to him. He was a sun-worshipper and was never happier than when he could relax in the hot sun in the minimum of clothing. A general feeling of contentment pervaded his whole being when he could lie in the sun, relaxed, preferably on a golden beach with the gentle sound of the lapping waves and in the distance the cry of sea-birds.

He did not see Ruth before he left for Spain, but phoned her the day before. His heart pounded uncomfortably as he waited, listening to the ringing tone. It was so long since he had heard her gentle voice with its sweet inflections and hint of sunny laughter. He could imagine her busy about the flat, then pausing as the phone rang and hurrying to answer it. Would she hope it was Anton? Or would she be expecting Gregg's voice at the other end of the line? He dreaded hearing disappointment in her voice. He had never imagined such a love as he felt for Ruth could exist. She was his life — and now there was no life for him, without her.

Suddenly the receiver was lifted and he closed his eyes against the brief spasm of pain as he heard that well-loved voice.'

'Ruth?' He forced himself to speak her name.

'Yes.'

'It's Anton.'

He heard her indrawn gasp of breath.

'Oh, hallo. How are you, Anton?' She spoke quickly, shyly.

'Fine,' he answered casually. 'I just phoned to let you know that I leave to-morrow morning.'

'Oh! I see. Will you be away long?' she asked politely, as though he were a stranger, when she longed to cry his name and tell him of her love for him, longed to ask him to come home to her.

'A month or so. Maybe longer. Everything all right with you?' He was eager to know whether she missed him, whether she was unhappy, and he could not keep a slight hint of eagerness out of his voice. But Ruth was so shaken by the sound of his voice, his sudden nearness, that she did not notice the inflection.

'Yes. Of course,' she replied proudly. So he thought she could not get along without him — the conceit of the man! She felt quite indignant.

'Good.' There was a pause. Anton thought angrily how stilted the conversation was. It seemed incredible that he was speaking to his wife. How cold she was, how aloof she sounded. Obviously there were no regrets for her part, she was not missing him at all and did not welcome his bothering her by telephone.

'Did Mark get in touch with you?'

'Yes, thank you.'

'Did he explain about the money — and the flat?'

'Yes. But you had no need to do anything like that, Anton. I am quite able to support myself — I did before we were married!'

'I know, Ruth. But I feel happier about you, knowing that you'll always have some money to your account.' So she even spurned his money.

'Of course you can easily spare it,' Ruth retorted. Her pride was hurt that he thought she would be comforted by money for his loss.

'That's beside the point.' He was determined not to let her ruffle his temper.

Ruth decided to change the subject. 'I hope you enjoy your holiday, Anton. Are you going by sea?' she asked. She wished she could feel some spiritual contact with this man, who was her husband, but seemed more like a stranger during this unnatural conversation.

'No, 'plane. I dislike long journeys.'

'You've flown before, haven't you?'

He nodded absentmindedly, then said quickly, 'Yes. Several times.'

'Well . . . ' There was a slight pause, then Ruth said: 'I hope you have a safe journey. Thank you for ringing me.'

'Ruth!' Anton cried. There was a moment's silence and he was afraid she had hung up.

Then, quietly, she said: 'Yes, Anton?'

'There's nothing you wanted to ask me?' he said stiltedly, longing to cry out his love.

'No. I don't think so.'

'Sure?' There was a silent plea in his question that she would give him the answer he wanted so much to hear.

'Yes, thank you. Quite sure. Well — good-bye, Anton.'

'Good-bye, Ruth.' He was reluctant to let her go, but there was nothing he could say to hold her. He replaced the receiver, sick at heart, and helped himself to a stiff drink. Then he sat down, glass in hand, and stared unseeingly at the far wall.

Meanwhile, Ruth buried her face in her hands. Tears coursed silently down her cheeks. Anton's voice, so cold and unfriendly, disinterested. He was probably anxious to put thoughts of Ruth behind him, anxious to get away to Spain to forget his wife in the arms of other women, Spanish beauties . . . Her thoughts trailed off.

★ ★ ★

The next morning, Ruth woke, early as always, and immediately thought of Anton; very soon now he would be leaving England, in a plane that would take him even farther away from her.

Never again would she hold him close, hear his dear voice, feel his strong arms about her and the heavy pounding of his heart as he drew her against him. She thought of him with a heavy heart and longed for him, for his love — though she had never possessed that, at least he had been fond of her and had shown her affection in his own way.

She threw back the covers and sat up. A sudden wave of nausea hit her and, startled, she sank down again. But she found each time she tried to sit up, so the sickness came. She lay for some time waiting for the feeling of nausea to abate, and finally managed to get out of bed, only to make her way unsteadily to the bathroom.

Some time later, Ruth managed to make herself a cup of hot, strong tea and a slice of toast, which was all that she felt she could stomach. She sat at the kitchen table, her head on her hand, feeling miserable and unwell.

It was not usual for Ruth to have bouts of sickness and her general health was good. She was worried. Then she remembered the faintness she had experienced only a few days ago — and with a sudden sinking of her heart she realized that possibly she was going to have a baby. She chided herself for not having suspected before. She calculated quickly.

'Oh, goodness!' she cried aloud. 'What will Anton say?' She knew that he would not welcome a child.

Suddenly she remembered that Anton wouldn't be interested. He was probably at this moment on his way to Spain — and she was here in England carrying his unborn child. She lifted her head proudly, elation filling her heart. At least, if she had lost Anton, no one could take his child away from her. She would have something of Anton that she could keep close to her for ever, cherish and love for the rest of her life.

But how much more wonderful it would be, she thought sadly, if Anton were with me now, and I could tell him that I am to have his son: how marvellous to have him with me through all the coming months, and then to be able to bring our child up together in a happy home.

Even if Anton were not enthusiastic about children, his own son would make him change his mind, Ruth felt — if things could be as she wished.

But she was determined that her son would not lack anything else because he would not know his father — would not have his father's guidance in life — would not be able to play with his 'daddy' as other little boys did. Ruth would have to be both mother and father and the task would be difficult — but not impossible.

Her heart felt lighter, knowing that she carried a child within her body. It had always been her wish to have children, especially to give Anton a son. Loving him as she did, she had imagined a son in his image, spent hours dreaming of happy days to come when she and Anton and their children would live in the country cottage that he planned to buy one day. Now those dreams were worthless. But she would still have his son.

She felt no fear that the child might not be a son: that was impossible. In her heart she knew this baby was a boy. He would have the same dark, well-shaped head with its arrogant lift, the brilliant impish blue eyes, the sensitive, long and tapering hands, and the fine, masculine body of his father. A boy as fine as his father, a boy she would be proud to call her son. A boy that not even Anton would be ashamed to know as his son, if ever there came a time when she told him.

* * *

Anton leaned back in his comfortable seat with a sigh born of well-being. It had been a pleasant luncheon, and it was even more pleasant to be speeding through the air with no worries, sure of getting to one's destination with the minimum of time and trouble.

He glanced at his watch: in just over an hour they would be in Madrid. And from there a short journey by car would take him to Castilio. It was some years since he had enjoyed a holiday in this small town, and now he remembered the experience with a stirring of excitement. His mind went back to the happy days he had spent at the little hotel and the Lopez family who owned it — how fond he had grown of them in such a short time.

The man who sat opposite Anton looked up from his magazine and, catching Anton's eyes, smiled. He was a tall man, roughly Anton's own build, with a pleasant face and dark, handsome eyes. He laid aside his magazine and took his cigarette-case from his breast pocket. With a friendly smile he leaned forward and offered the cigarettes to Anton.

'Care to join me?'

Experiencing a sudden sensation of warmth at the friendly gesture, Anton nodded. 'Thanks.'

'Madrid bound?' his companion asked him, as he flicked a lighter.

'Yes — but I'm going on to Castilio

almost immediately.'

'Charming little place.' He handed Anton a card, which he took from his wallet, and introduced himself. 'My name is John Newman. I live in Madrid — permanently, for my firm, with occasional trips to England. If you are in the city at any time during your stay in Spain, I should be glad if you would join me for dinner one evening.'

'I should be delighted. I shall certainly be in Madrid at some time during my visit. By the way, my name is Anton' — he hesitated almost imperceptibly — 'Marshall.' He could not have explained his reasons for giving a false name. It had been an impulse.

John Newman had not noticed the pause. Living in Spain for most of the year, apart from rare trips to England when, after completing his business affairs, he made his way to his brother's farm in Cornwall, he seldom visited London theatres, had little interest in drama, so he failed to recognize the man he talked with as Anton Radinov, the famous actor.

The two men chatted amicably together for the rest of the journey. When they reached the airport, they went through the customs together, then had coffee and cigarettes in the lounge while waiting for Anton's hired car to arrive. They shook hands warmly on parting, having discovered in each other a warm and likeable personality. Already a friendship had been struck up between them.

'Now don't forget. You have my card and I shall expect to hear from you,' John reminded him, as he saw him to the car, complete with luggage. 'We'll make it a gala evening.'

Anton laughed. 'I'll depend on you to make all the arrangements. All right, John — I'll definitely be in touch with you soon.' He sank back into his seat and the car drove off. John Newman stood looking after the car, a hope in his heart that it wasn't the last he had seen of his new friend.

Anton was looking forward to renewing his acquaintance with Castilio, but he was afraid of disappointment. Perhaps it was a mistake to try to recapture old emotions: it was mainly nostalgia that was bringing him back to this small Spanish town. He warned himself to expect changes.

He strode into the familiar, white, sprawling hotel — which was hardly larger than an inn — and looked about him. To his pleasant surprise, Pedro, the old man who was not only doorkeeper, wine-waiter, bell-boy, boot-boy, but most other of the necessary hotel appendages as well, was sitting as he had always done — sprawled in a wicker chair, his weary old eyes closed, his black hair even thinner and greasier than Anton had remembered it to be. Anton grinned. A little of the old Castilio still remained then. He strode over to Pedro and shook him gently.

'*Madre Dios!*' The old man sat up with a startled exclamation. Then, fully awake, he looked into Anton's smiling face. 'Mother of God! It is the Señor Anton!!' He jumped up and ran into a back room, an excited torrent of Spanish bursting from his lips. Within moments, Anton was surrounded by Papa and Mama. Lopez, their two sons, Juan and Fernando, their daughter Lolita and her husband Davos, and two small brown, plump children, Lolita's babies. They were all excited at sight of Anton and could not make him welcome enough. Laughing, gesticulating, talking rapidly in Spanish, they enveloped him with warmth and friendship.

Very soon he was sitting in the back parlour, as of old, with the long strings of onions hanging from the rafters, the strong stench of garlic prevading the room, and coffee bubbling on the old black stove. Wine was produced with great ceremony.

The babies, shy of the stranger, held back at first, but before long they were clustered about his knee, listening intently to his every word, studying his every expression.

'Aren't you married yet?' Anton turned to the eldest son, Juan.

'No, no! He is still breaking the hearts of all our young maidens,' his father answered for him, a broad smile on his face. 'They love his rough country ways.'

'And Fernando?' Anton asked.

The young boy to whom he now spoke — who was perhaps twenty — flushed: 'I am to be married soon,' he said shyly.

'You will stay for the wedding — *si?*' cried Mama.

'When is it to be?'

'A week to-morrow.'

'Then of course I shall be here. Who is the bride?'

'Our son marries Maria Tendroz — you remember?' Papa said proudly. 'It is a good match.'

'Pretty Maria with the long black pigtails and the shy brown eyes. Is she old enough to marry?' Anton asked in

214

surprise. 'I forget it is six years since I was here.'

'She is seventeen — and her pigtails are gone.'

'You will want to rest after your journey. Pedro, show the Señor Anton to the best room in the house.' Mama suddenly remembered her duties as a hostess.

Anton rose, his eyes suddenly warm with affection. 'You have given me such a welcome that I am sorry to have waited so long before coming back to Castilio.' He slipped an arm around Fernando's shoulders. 'I look forward to seeing you wed Maria — remind me to buy you the best wedding present I can find in Madrid!' He dropped his arm and turned to Mama, slipping an arm about her ample waist. 'Mama, it has been a long time to be away from you. I missed you most of all — and your wonderful cooking. Do you think your husband would mind if I stole a kiss to prove how glad I am to be back?'

'He is too old to care!' she laughed, her big body shaking. Anton bent his head and gave her a resounding kiss on both cheeks.

'Not too old!' cried Papa in mock anger. '*Madre Dios!* I can still compete with your young and dashing new cavalier.' Saying this, he flung both arms around Mama and gave her a hearty, full-blooded kiss, to the accompaniment of cheers of encouragement from his sons.

Mama pushed him away, gasping for breath, laughing. 'It is the wine,' she said to Anton in explanation. 'It has gone to his head. He does not drink so much these days.'

Papa poured another glass and raised it high.

'To-day we have good cause to drink the wine.'

Anton looked around him, a smile transforming his face. Everything was as it used to be. Nothing had changed, here in Castilio, at least.

Later, in his room — the best room

216

in the house, as Mama had promised — Anton, unpacking, realized that he had hardly thought of Ruth at all for some time. But now, at the memory of his lovely young wife, he felt a pang of regret for the happiness they could have known together, if he had waited to earn her love before they married. He had always been aware of her love for him, a love he knew he had never merited — but marriage to the man she cared for so much had not brought her happiness. Anton had destroyed her love with his thoughtless treatment of her. He knew it — why else her heartrending cry: 'I wish I'd never married you!'

Anton took a cigarette from his gold case with a quick, impatient movement, lighted it, and wandered to the window, where he stood looking out on the dusty street, lit occasionally by lights from the windows of the houses.

Had he been hasty in leaving Ruth? Or was he justified in his feeling that if Ruth had said such a thing then she was too unhappy to continue in the way of life he had chosen for her much longer. If so, the best thing he could do in Ruth's own interests was to end that way of life as quickly as possible.

He did not doubt that Ruth would divorce him. He knew that Mark Gantry would do all in his power to help Ruth, if only for the sake of his friendship with Anton.

Anton felt suddenly that if he never saw Ruth again he would perhaps have the strength to go through life without her, without the happiness she could bring him. But once more to look into her candid, beautiful grey eyes, to see her sunny face light up with happiness, to smell the fragrance of her corn-coloured hair, would mean that he would spend the rest of his life longing for her, wishing that once more he could have her love.

He watched a peasant leading a dusty donkey through the streets, but his eye did not take in the sight. His thoughts were on his own foolishness in the past, the waste of his life in idle affairs, the stupid search for pleasure and sensual excitement.

Common sense told him that some of his life had not been wasted — for many years now he had brought drama and fine acting into the lives of many people. He had written hundreds of articles on the theatre and its history — had written also two fine plays. Successes in the theatrical world, but as far as Anton himself was concerned, they had fallen far short of the standard he set. He knew that he possessed more depth of genius within him that had not yet seen the light of day — but something seemed to elude him. He had never known true satisfaction with his work. He had failed to give his labours the true devotion that he knew they needed. Rona — and others whose favours he had enjoyed — bitterly he realized now that they had all done their share in distracting him from his writing and his acting.

When he married Ruth he had been sure in some obscure way that he was doing the only right thing that he had ever done. He had known that through Ruth he would find his real genius. But everything had gone wrong — he did not deny that it was his own fault.

With a sigh he turned from the window. Well, whatever genius he did possess, he would have to discover it now on his own. There was no longer Ruth: he had spurned the gift the Gods sent him — so they had taken it back.

* * *

Despite his inner depression the days flew quickly for Anton. He found contentment with the Lopez family, and enjoyed the simple life.

He was pleased to meet Lolita, the Lopez eldest daughter, again. During his last visit to Castilio he had carried on a mild affair with this dark-eyed Spanish girl, with the understanding on both sides that it ended on his return to England. Now she was married and had two babies. As Anton had guessed, a lot of her beauty had waned as she grew older and she was plumper. But marriage and motherhood suited her, Anton decided, studying her with her husband Davos, her babies around her feet. She had been delighted to see Anton, but not so pleased that she caused her husband an instant's jealousy. Indeed, she introduced Davos to Anton with such a proud light in her eyes that it was obvious there was no other man for her, nor ever could be.

The wedding between the young couple, Fernando and Maria, was a festive occasion. Wine flowed freely, so did talk and laughter. Food was plentiful and Mama bustled about, seeing that everyone was well supplied with everything. She was very proud of her handsome son, dressed in his wedding finery, radiating happiness from his dark eyes as he watched the progress of his bride from group to group. Maria was young and pretty, her long dark hair was piled high on her head and she wore the wedding mantilla with such purity of expression, yet with such obvious childish delight, that she was a joy to watch.

A few days after the wedding, Anton decided to go to Madrid, look up his new friend, John Newman, spend a few days in the city, and then return to Castilio with presents for his friends. He had not been in touch with John since their parting at the airport, but he looked forward to meeting him again.

The first thing he did on arrival in the city was to phone John, who gave him a warm welcome and immediately made plans for dinner that evening and a tour of the few good night-clubs. Anton agreed instantly and with pleasure.

He booked in at an excellent hotel, smiling as he compared its grand exterior to that of the small Lopez inn: he knew which he instinctively preferred. The large suite he occupied left no room for comparisons with his room in Castilio. It was the best suite in the hotel.

Anton had picked up his mail at the Madrid branch of his bank. Now he ran through it idly. A letter from Sol Flavek, asking him about his plans — how long he would be in Spain — agitating about rehearsals for his new play. Two from Rona, light, casual, but with an undercurrent of ambiguity; she had heard of his trip to Spain and was hurt that he had not let her know. She would have been delighted to accompany him. Usual gossip about their mutual friends. Anton threw both letters aside impatiently, sickened by the thoughts of the intimacy he had known with Rona and determined to be rid of her cloying charms in the future. A letter from his bank manager — official, unimportant and uninteresting. A letter from Mark Gantry, giving him details of his meeting with Ruth — adding a rider to the effect that he was surprised at Anton, allowing such a sincere and lovely girl to slip through his fingers, and relying on their long friendship to forgive him if he were impertinent, but what had happened? Would Anton write and explain?

Anton threw the mail on his bed, exasperated. Not one of the letters made him feel disposed to answer them. He would not worry if he never saw Rona again; he was in no mood to be harried by Flavek with regard to his dramatic future; Mark's letter had induced a strong sense of depression and futility; the letter from his bank manager only informed him how exceptionally good was his monetary status — money! when Anton wanted nothing but Ruth, her love and their mutual happiness.

Suddenly, on a mad impulse, he snatched the telephone from its cradle and sent a cable.

By doing this he threw up his entire dramatic career, all claim to his wife, all interest in his finances.

10

Gregg was one of the first to have the news. A friend of his was a reporter on the *Daily Echo*, and Jamie Jackson rang Gregg early in the morning.

'Gregg! Have you heard the news? Shocking affair! But of course, you wouldn't have heard. News just came over the ticker tape.'

'What news?'

'Sorry.' Jamie was always a bit vague. 'Anton Radinov is dead. Sorry to have to break it to you, he's a friend of yours, I know.'

'Dead? How?' Gregg sat up in bed sharply, shocked.

'Fever — in some outlandish village in Spain.' There was a pause. Gregg was too astonished to speak. 'I'm sorry, Gregg,' Jamie went on, 'he was a pal of yours; he'll be a loss to many people. It'll be in the papers this morning, but

I thought you'd like to know first.'

'Thanks, Jamie. I appreciate your thought.'

Gregg rang off, shocked and grieved. Anton — of all people! When Ruth heard, she would be frantic with grief. He leapt out of bed. He must get to Ruth before she heard the news from any other source but him.

He paused to buy a paper on the way to the flat, but it only confirmed what he already knew. In large black letters across the front page were the words:

FAMOUS ACTOR DIES IN SPAIN

and below:

Anton Radinov meets his death in tragic circumstances

He did not stop to read any more. Ruth was preparing breakfast when Gregg arrived. Her morning paper, which had already been delivered, was still on the mat, and Gregg picked it

226

up with relief. He rang the bell and she came to the door, looking wan and unhappy, surprised that she should have such an early caller.

'Why, Gregg!' she exclaimed. 'Come in.' She stood back and he went in, unsmiling, dreading his self-set task. 'You're very early. Did I expect you — had I forgotten you were coming?' She smiled up at him.

'No, Ruth. I simply had to see you.' He hesitated, anxious to put off the moment of revelation. 'Do I smell fresh coffee?'

'Of course.' She hastened to give him a cup, wondering at his grim expression. 'You see, I've had to teach myself how to use the percolator,' she added, with a wry smile.

He nodded without answering, and sat down on the settee.

'Is anything wrong, Gregg?' Ruth asked anxiously.

He put his cup down, untasted, and took her hands in his. 'Ruth, you'll have to be very brave, my dear. I've bad news for you — very bad.'

She went white. 'Anton! Something's happened to him!'

'Darling Ruth, you've got to be brave. I hate to tell you, but I couldn't leave you to find out alone.'

'Tell me, Gregg.' She trembled, but her voice was quiet, and she looked at him calmly.

'Anton is dead, Ruth.'

She drew a quick, gasping breath. She felt stunned. Dead! How could it be. He had been so alive only a few days ago, had spoken to her — he had been well then.

'But — I don't understand. How? I mean, he wasn't ill. No one told me he was ill.' She sounded like a confused child.

'It was fever. He died in Spain.'

She suddenly crumpled. He put his arms around her to save her fall; she was in a dead faint. Tenderly he laid her on the settee. How deathly pale she was. What had she done to deserve so much pain, Gregg asked bitterly.

He went for water, then decided that brandy would be better and found some in the cocktail cabinet.

As Ruth came back from oblivion, she was conscious of a great grief, a heaviness of her spirit. The man she loved so dearly was dead. Even if she had lost him as a husband, at least he had been alive and well. But this — death was so terrible, so final. Why? Why? Why such futile waste of a fine and brilliant man?

The brandy brought her to her senses. She looked at Gregg absently for a moment or two, then realization came more fully and with it the tears. Gregg held her close, the deep shudders of her body finding an echo in his heart; the warm bitter tears coursed down her cheeks. His heart went out to her. If only there was some way to comfort her.

He had always known of her adoration for Anton: that no matter what her husband did, she would always have loved him with an eternal love. If they had been divorced and Gregg could have persuaded Ruth to marry him, in her heart she would still have been Anton's wife, and nothing would have changed her.

Some time later Ruth was more composed, and asked Gregg to read her the article in the newspaper. She closed her eyes against the pain a few times, but when he would have laid the paper aside, she motioned him to carry on.

There was a long article on Anton, his career and his brilliance: as much as was known of the mysterious fever from which he had died. They still knew so little — the bare facts had reached them by cable from a man named John Newman.

Gregg insisted that Ruth should have a mild sedative and try to sleep while he made a few enquiries to see what else he could discover. She agreed listlessly.

When she woke, some hours later, Gregg was with her, his face drawn and unhappy.

The first question she asked startled him.

'What will they do with him? They won't let him be buried in Spain, will they? Won't I ever see him again?' Her voice was strange, her eyes unseeing, and Gregg felt a sudden anxiety.

'I understand that arrangements have already been made in Spain for his burial.' He spoke gently. 'It's the best thing. In such a hot country swift burials are necessary, especially where a person has died of fever. It wouldn't be wise to bring him home.'

'I must see him!' she insisted.

He shook his head firmly. 'It's impossible, Ruth.'

She began to cry softly.

Gregg was silent.

'How could they identify him?' she wanted to know.

'By his personal papers, I guess.'

'There couldn't be a mistake?'

'I don't know, Ruth.' He frowned. He had been unable to contact the man who had sent the cable: connections

231

had been bad and the news agency he spoke to seemed to know little more about the incident than they had already made public. They had assured Gregg that they had received the cable, that it was authentic — enquiries had been made in Castilio and it appeared that an Englishman visiting the village had been stricken with fever and died. His death had been registered in the name of Anton Radinov. Other details of his identity tallied. They regretted that it would be impossible for anyone from England to reach Castilio before the burial. In such a small place, in a hot country, especially with a fever victim, burial was swift.

Gregg shook his head. 'I checked carefully, Ruth: there is no mistake. How could there be? Anton is dead. Ruth, dear, let's not talk about it for a little while. I don't think you should discuss it — I hate to see you upset.'

She turned her face away. 'Don't you see, Gregg, I have to talk about it. I can't — I daren't — *not* talk about it. It isn't possible that Anton is really — dead!' Her hand flew to her mouth as if to stifle the word. 'He was always so vital, so alive,' she went on, her voice flat, expressionless. 'He simply can't be dead. There isn't any sense in it. It's a futile waste of life.'

'I agree — but life is like that, Ruth. Senseless in lots of ways, at the time. It's only much later that one sees the reason for these things.'

'Reason? Where is the reason in Anton's death?' Ruth cried. 'I loved him — I tried to be a good wife to him. Perhaps I did wrong to resent the way he lived his life — to try to change him. But I always loved him — now I've lost him. Why, Gregg? Why? Tell me the reason!'

Gregg fumbled with his cigarette-case — he did not wish to meet her eyes. He had no answer for her. But she continued to gaze at him enquiringly, waiting: so he mumbled something about it being 'an act of God'.

She caught him up on his words instantly. 'An act of God? — to cut short his life. Such a man! He was brilliant, a genius . . . '

'Ruth, don't distress yourself,' he reproached her anxiously.

'But it's true, Gregg,' she cried. 'Surely you feel as I do, that there is no reason at all why Anton should die now — he was still young, he had a lot to accomplish yet.'

'Death is neither discriminate nor reasonable. Anton is dead. That's the bare truth. You must accept it, and try to make a life for yourself without him.' He paused, and his eyes were suddenly grim. 'If you think I am being hard — or cruel, Ruth, just try to remember that I loved him too. He was more than a friend to me, and I feel his loss keenly — I resent losing him almost as much as you do. But life has to go on, and Anton would prefer it that way. I'm only trying to help you. You know that.'

Ruth nodded. She did know. She

realized he was right, but her initial grief was still too great for her to accept Anton's death easily.

She was astounded and shocked the next morning when she opened her paper and read the headlines. The newspapers were still playing up the tragic death of Anton Radinov.

SECRET ENGAGEMENT OF DEAD ACTOR. LOVELY SOCIETY SOPHISTICATE ADMITS MARRIAGE PLANS WITH ANTON RADINOV

There was a photograph of Anton and Rona, taken in a night-club; they sat smiling happily into each other's eyes; Anton's hand tightly clasped the girl's.

Ruth read on, amazed and angry.

'Rona Grant-Hawkeley told our special reporter last night that she had been secretly engaged to the famous actor who was reported to have died this week of a fever in Spain. They had been friends for some years, and planned to marry in the autumn of this year.

'For private reasons of their own, the engagement had been kept secret, and therefore is news not only to the public and the press, but also to the close friends of the couple.

'Miss Grant-Hawkeley is naturally deeply grieved at the loss of her famous fiancé, Anton Radinov . . .'

Ruth did not read any further. Seized by a sudden storm of anger, she threw the paper across the room. How dare she? How dare this cheap sophisticate soil Anton's name with a pack of lies.

She waited eagerly for Gregg's arrival. When he came, she greeted him impatiently.

'Have you seen the papers?' she demanded. 'Have you seen the lies that Rona has dared to have printed?'

He nodded. 'Yes, I have. I suppose she thought herself safe enough. Who is to deny the truth of her statements? It's no secret that he's been escorting her for months — it's possible that they could have been engaged as far as the public's concerned. Anton would have had several reasons for keeping an engagement quiet.'

'*I* am to deny it,' Ruth cried. 'I won't let that woman get away with this. Gregg, I want you to phone the papers and tell them the truth. Tell them that I am Anton's *wife* — and that I am to have his child!'

Gregg drew a sharp breath. 'Did you say child?'

'Yes, I did. I'm going to have a baby. Ring them, Gregg, tell them.' He stared at her in surprise. She grew impatient. 'Well, don't look so astonished. Women do have babies, you know. Why shouldn't I have one?'

'What unbelievably bad luck!' Gregg exclaimed.

'Bad luck? That's a strange reaction, I must say!'

He came to her side and took her hands.

'Not really. I admire you so much,

Ruth. Where do you get your courage? You make an unhappy marriage, discover you're pregnant *after* your husband walks out on you — and before you can tell him the news and perhaps save your marriage, he dies in a faraway country. Believe me, Ruth, if Anton had known about the baby he would never have left you. To cap it all, you find out from the press that according to some cheap seeker after publicity, he's engaged to her — but you don't even turn a hair. And you wonder why I say — bad luck!'

She smiled at him. 'What should I do? Go into hysterics? That would be bad for the baby. Please ring the press, Gregg.'

'You bet I will. Rona is in for a shock — I'd love to see her face when she reads our comeback to her little scheme!' He laughed a little grimly and reached for the telephone. Within a few moments he was speaking to Jamie Jackson.

'That you, Jamie? Listen, this is

Gregg. You did me a favour yesterday — to-day I'm doing you one. I've got a scoop for you — red hot! What? Oh, wait a minute! Give me time. Will it catch the midday edition . . . ?'

A thought struck Ruth as he said this, and she laid a hand on his sleeve quickly. He raised an enquiring eyebrow. 'Just a sec, Jamie. Hold on, will you.' He put his hand over the mouthpiece. 'What is it, Ruth. Changed your mind?'

'No. I think it's a better idea to let the news hold over until to-morrow. Give the whole country time to read Rona's story — it will add to her discomfiture when they read my story to-morrow!'

Gregg grinned. 'You do mean to have your revenge, don't you?' He turned back to his friend. 'Right, Jamie, here it is. At the moment, I'm in Anton Radinov's flat. Yes, his flat. Standing by me is — wait for it! — his *wife*! Yes, you heard right. His wife. That's right. Married late

February — a secret wedding. Yes, secret — must be catching, these secret affairs — but I can assure you, Jamie, this is the truth. I was at the wedding.' He paused a moment. 'Description of the bride? Photographs? Oh, that can wait. I'll contact you later. Keep this until to-morrow's editions, will you.' He explained what Ruth had said, evidently in reply to a question, and Ruth could hear the reporter's delighted laughter at the other end. 'Brilliant, eh?' Gregg went on. 'Let me see — they were married at Caxton Hall, February 24th. Her name was Ruth Strong. Oh, one other thing, Jamie. An even better piece of news to please your editor — Anton Radinov's posthumous child will be born towards the end of the year.' He paused to give his words more weight. 'Right, Jamie. I can trust you to play it up. This is an exclusive. Yes, that's the advantage of having friends in the know.' He grinned. 'I shall expect some real fun and games from the

Echo in the morning. So long, I'll be ringing you later.' He hung up and turned to Ruth with sparkling eyes. 'Well?'

'It sounded good. You were so excited.' Ruth laughed at him affectionately. 'And your friend seemed amused.'

'He was. He has no love for Rona's type!'

* * *

The press seized on the news. Naturally the *Echo* was first with the startling revelations, and they made much of it. All England was talking of the affair within a few days.

Rona was terribly shocked. Anton had kept the secret of his marriage well. She did the only possible thing she could to save her face.

An urgent phone call to Jay Scott brought him to her flat by midday, the day the news broke. Rona was floating around in a pale lilac negligée, as was usual at that time of day; her beautiful

241

hair was well groomed, her lovely face carefully made up.

Léonie, her maid, announced Jay. Rona had been seated at the piano, idly strumming the latest dance tunes, but she turned as he entered.

'Jay!' She greeted him with outstretched hand, a warmth in her eyes and smile. He came over to her and clasped her hand for the briefest second.

'Hallo, Rona. How do you contrive to look so lovely so early in the day?' he asked dryly, and she had the fleeting impression that he was mocking her. They had known each other for years, and he had long since lost all illusions about her.

She smiled. 'You're such an adept at saying the right things. I'll ring for coffee — or would you prefer a drink?' She crossed the room and pressed the bell to summon Léonie.

'Coffee, I think, I've a headache — ask Léonie to bring some aspirin, will you?'

'Of course. Poor darling, were you on a binge last night? Come and sit down.' She led him to the elegant but comfortable Regency sofa, and they sat down together. 'I'll massage your temples. People say I have healing hands — is it green fingers?'

Jay grinned. 'No. That's for growing plants and flowers.'

'Oh!' She laughed. 'Trust me to get it wrong.'

Léonie entered silently.

'Coffee, please, Léonie — and aspirin for Mr. Scott.' The maid nodded and turned to go. 'Oh, there was something else,' Rona went on. She paused a moment, thinking. 'I remember. The cigarette box is empty.'

'Very well, Miss Rona.' She left as silently as she had entered.

Rona turned her slim, lithe body towards Jay and her long white fingers reached to caress his forehead, moving gently to the nape of his neck. He grinned and caught her hand.

'Being 'the hand that heals' doesn't

suit you. My headache will go, given time. Tell me why you were so insistent on seeing me? Were you lonely? Did you want to elope — and I was the first man you thought of?'

'Darling! Don't deceive yourself. I've turned to you in trouble — and nothing else.'

'Trouble wouldn't mean this business of you and Anton Radinov?' he asked slyly, knowing the answer full well.

She nodded. 'You've seen the papers, then?' She twined her fingers together on her lap and played restlessly with her beautiful rings.

'I've been following them closely, my dear. When one's dear friends are discussed by the whole of the country, one feels honour bound to take an interest.' He frowned suddenly at the restless movement of her hands, and laid his own right hand on hers with a swift, reassuring gesture. 'Why all the lies, Rona?' he asked gently.

She coloured, surprising herself and her companion. It was a long time since the self-assured and sophisticated young woman had been so easily disarmed.

'They aren't necessarily lies!' she retorted, and drew her hands from his. 'How do you know my story isn't true — Anton told me nothing about his marriage, and if he had asked me to marry him, I should have agreed, and I would have considered us engaged.'

Jay ignored this tirade. 'You don't seem very concerned over the loss of your 'fiancé', Rona. Contrary to what the press says.'

'You know darn well that Anton and I weren't engaged — Anton was much too clever,' she said bitterly. 'I'd have given anything to marry him, but I didn't think he was the marrying type.' She bowed her head slightly.

Jay was silent for a moment. Then, with his fingers lightly lifting her chin, 'Rona, my dear, you're deceiving yourself. You may have imagined you loved Anton and wanted to marry him — what you really wanted was his name and a share in his limelight . . . '

'Nonsense! I have limelight of my own — and my name is quite good enough on its own without being coupled with Anton's!' she interrupted.

'Then why couple it?' he asked slyly. 'Why won't you admit your motives — you wanted to see the faces of your friends when they discovered that you'd pulled it off, after all.'

'I know a certain section of our crowd were betting on the outcome,' cried Rona. 'I would have succeeded — Anton and I would have been married in time, but this cheap little golddigger, whom no one has ever heard of, stepped in first. Who is she, anyway? God knows what Anton was thinking of to marry her! Tell me, Jay, Why? Why did he marry that little nobody when . . . ' She stopped abruptly.

' . . . When he could have had you for the asking?' Jay finished.

Rona stared at him. 'You really believe that!'

'But of course. The facts are there,

Rona. You don't imagine she trapped him into marriage — a man like Anton?' he asked incredulously.

Rona shook her head. Jay was right. If Anton had married this girl, he did it willingly and because he wanted a 'nobody' as a wife.

Léonie entered with a tray: a few moments later, Rona was pouring steaming coffee into the two cups.

She helped herself to a cigarette from the newly filled box and Jay reached forward for the table lighter — a nude statue of the Goddess Diana. He raised his eyebrows.

'An appropriate little ornament for you to have around,' he told her with a grin, as he held the flame to her cigarette.

She shrugged. 'Diana the Huntress? I expect that's what Anton thought when he bought her for me.'

'Oh — a gift from Anton.'

'One of Anton's gifts,' she corrected him, with a secret little smile quirking her lips.

'You sound like a kept woman!' Jay snapped in sudden annoyance.

Rona was unperturbed. 'Oh, no, Jay. You're wrong. Anton never had to pay for his favours where I was concerned.'

'That I can imagine!'

Rona stubbed her cigarette with impatience. 'But why we're sitting here fencing with words, I don't know. Look here, Jay, you realize I'm in a jam over this affair of Anton being already married. Unless I retract quickly from my part in the affair, or distract their attention with some other news, I shall be the laughing stock of the country. I can't face that. So what am I going to do?'

'In Heaven's name, why ask me?' Jay protested.

'Whom else can I ask? You're one of the most quickwitted men I know — surely you can think of some way out, some counter movement. Please help me.' She laid her hand on his arm, pleading, smiling a little helplessly.

'The only thing I can suggest is for

you to marry someone else,' he replied, after a few moments.

'Who? In any case I don't want to marry anyone. Why should I?'

'No one's making you marry, Rona — but it would make a good story, a nice red herring. Accuse some reporter of putting two and two together and making five, just because you and Anton spent some time in each other's company — oh, in a discreet way, of course. Deny all knowledge of a secret engagement and tell them the real 'truth' — that you're really engaged to someone quite different. They'd probably swallow that.'

'Perhaps.' Rona mused for a few seconds. 'It sounds a good idea, Jay. Darling, I knew you'd think of something. Now the thing to decide is — who?'

'M'm?' Jay replied absent-mindedly, his thoughts elsewhere.

'I said — who? Who will agree to an engagement without explanation — just for convenience?'

'There must be one amongst your many men friends who would willingly play the part of your fiancé.'

'Oh, of course,' Rona replied impatiently. 'But they'd want to marry me after a while. I couldn't brush any of them off with an engagement of convenience. They'd hold me to the promise.'

'Well, then, you need a man who isn't mad about you, and who certainly wouldn't dream of marrying you. I know just the man!'

'You do? That's wonderful, Jay. Who is he?'

'Me!' he replied, deliberate and grammarless. Rona stared at him in astonishment. 'Are you serious?'

'Why shouldn't I be?'

'But you've a reputation as a woman-hater!'

'A man can change his mind. Who would blame me for changing it to marry you? In any case, I'm not marrying you, really, am I?'

Rona considered it. 'You know,' she

said thoughtfully, 'it really is a very good idea. After all, we can be sure of it being merely platonic!'

'Exactly how I feel.'

She pouted. 'Although I rather resent the fact that you aren't mad about me. I like my men to adore me.'

'I know you do. That's why a change will be good for you!'

She laughed. 'You win. You really are a pet, Jay. I can't think of anyone who would do so much for me.' She gave him a brief, fleeting kiss on his cheek.

'Now, Rona. Strictly platonic!' he reminded her, grinning, his eyes laughing mischievously into hers.

'When you look like that, darling, I'm not sure I want it that way,' she murmured softly.

He stood up abruptly. 'That's my exit line. I warn you, Rona, whenever you start getting romantic about me, I shall walk out. So curb your ideas right from the beginning. I refuse to be another of your conquests.'

The press the following day carried a newer story: they were thoroughly enjoying themselves. It was a long time since the papers had had such a field day.

RONA GRANT-HAWKELEY DENIES
ENGAGEMENT TO DEAD ACTOR

'It was announced to-day by Miss Rona Grant-Hawkeley, the famous and beautiful socialite daughter of Sir Iain and Lady Grant-Hawkeley, that the story of her romance with Anton Radinov was completely without foundation. As our readers will remember, we reported in this paper the amazing news of a secret engagement between the brilliant actor, victim of a fever epidemic in Spain, and Miss Grant-Hawkeley.

'It appears that the story was spread as a practical joke, and this paper must offer its sincere apologies to Mrs. Anton Radinov for any humiliation or embarrassment she may have suffered because of the false report.

'During Miss Grant-Hawkeley's interview with our reporter, she told him of the engagement that does exist between herself and the well-known theatrical critic, Mr. Jay Scott. It appears that they have been engaged for some months, a fact that only a few close friends were aware of, and they plan to marry later this year.'

Rona and Jay toasted the success of their 'red herring' that evening when they dined together, and a wonderful expensive diamond solitaire sparkled on the third finger of Rona's left hand.

11

John Newman stubbed his cigarette with an impatient movement. Anton watched him closely. It was too late to regret his action; the following morning all the English papers would carry the news of his reported death. He had known that John would resent Anton's high-handed use of his name as the sender of the cable, but felt sure that when he fully understood the reasons for that cable, he would forgive him.

'Why *my* name?' John asked now. 'Why not simply invent a name — any name? I shall be asked to confirm the cable. How can I explain the facts of a death that didn't even take place?'

Anton sat back in his armchair and crossed one knee over the other with a studied air of nonchalance. 'Use your imagination,' he suggested.

'Very easy for you to say that,' John

retorted. 'I should think your own imagination could do with a little curbing.' His eyes were dark with annoyance and faint lines of temper were evident about his mouth. He strode across the room and helped himself to another cigarette from the box on the table. Anton, who was idly turning the table-lighter between his long, artistic fingers, flicked into life the bright flame and held it to John's cigarette. 'Seriously, Anton, didn't you think twice about the whole thing?'

'No,' Anton admitted. 'I agree with you that I was foolish, that it was a mad impulse, and I quite sympathize with your irritation.'

John raised his eyes to heaven. 'Irritation! That's an understatement.' He fell silent, thinking of the pleasure he had felt at meeting this man again. He had sensed his warm and vital personality and admired him, had felt a kinship with him that he had never experienced before for any man but his brothers. He had wondered if Anton would follow up their chance meeting on the journey from England; when they met that evening for dinner, John had noticed his new friend's air of preoccupation, the sense of strain about him. They had dined alone and conversation had not flagged, although John knew it was an effort for his companion when obviously something was on his mind. At Anton's request the two men had returned to John's hotel room. In explanation, Anton had said that he wanted to talk to him, needed his help in a personal matter. That had been nearly two hours ago and still he had not felt capable of offering help. Anton's air of indifference to his action and the consequences that were sure to follow had rebuffed John.

He glanced now at Anton and took him off his guard. There was a look of vulnerability about him, of depression and loss, that made Anton's whole personality seem different, and suddenly John's irritation faded. He said, more gently: 'This is the sort of thing you would do — wild and reckless. When we first met I had a premonition that you would involve me in some kind of trouble, but I didn't feel worried. I'm not really worried now; I was annoyed with you, but that seems to have worn off. Now I want to help you. You asked me for help and I'm prepared to give it — I don't yet know in what way, but whatever you want me to do, Anton, I will do it.'

There was a sudden light in Anton's eyes, admiring, thankful, affectionate — all these things and more that John could not describe. 'I felt sure I could rely on you. Try to understand my motives, John. Sometimes a man like me feels he can't go on in the life he has chosen for himself — that he is failing himself and others at every turn of the road. Then a lesser man commits suicide or slinks away into the mists of nonentity — but a man such as I am chooses a more difficult path. He takes a new identity, kicks over the traces of his past life, leaves behind all that has ever meant anything to him, and prepares to make a new start in an entirely different field.'

John listened, quietly smoking, his big muscular body tense. He could not put a name to the feeling he had for this man, but he knew that he and Anton were more than friends, although they were comparative strangers, that neither would ever fail the other. It had been a strange story that Anton had told him, but nevertheless John trusted him and knew that, strange though Anton's actions may be, he had felt himself justified in them.

'What field are you planning to start in?' he asked, as Anton stopped speaking, and his thoughts were far ahead, rapidly making plans.

'That's where I'm asking your help,' admitted Anton candidly. 'You know about my past life, I've told you all I've done . . .'

'You've told me that you were in the theatre, that you're an actor of some repute and standing, that you've also tried your hand at writing plays and articles and had some success; that you've made plenty of money, but that you were born into it, anyway, so you've never known poverty or really hard manual work. You've hinted at the many women you've known, though you've said nothing about marriage, so I must assume you've always been a bachelor gay.' Anton would have spoken then, to tell him of Ruth, but something made him change his mind, and John did not notice the involuntary movement. He went on: 'I gather you've led a social life that was more than hectic, that you have been very much in the public eye. I suppose all that sort of thing to be very boring, but I've never experienced it, so I'm no judge.' John paused for a moment. 'I can understand why you want a new life — all I've just mentioned is very superficial for a man like you. I believe you have more depth of character than one would think from this summary of your life. You have been wasting your time . . . '

A semblance of pride stirred in Anton. 'The critics wouldn't agree with you. Some consider that I am a great actor, that with my fine ability and insight into my work I have brought convincing drama into the lives of many.'

'Do you think they won't find another great actor to take your place? Do you think that if you had never lived the theatre would have been that much poorer?' There was no irony in John's voice.

Anton considered for a moment. Then he shook his head. 'Of course I don't. You're right, John, I have a great deal too much conceit, too much faith in myself.'

'A man can never have enough faith in himself,' John corrected slowly. 'Without faith we are nothing. But the conceit is unnecessary. But you have had only the conceit and never the faith: otherwise you would not have a sense of failure. If you feel that you have failed, Anton, then you have lost faith in your own capabilities; it is time to start again with renewed faith and hope next time for a measure of success in your own eyes as well as other peoples'.'

'That's what I want to do. I told you, I want to kick over the traces, start a new life and make a real go of it this time. It isn't enough to have public acclaim that I'm wonderful and successful, I want to feel it myself and until I do I shall never be content, never know that I have fulfilled myself.' He drew a breath, looked at John with the faintest hint of diffidence in his brilliant blue eyes, then added: 'My real ambition is to write something really worthwhile, not flimsy plays or prosy articles, but something that will justify my living, something that will be remembered long after I am forgotten as a man.'

John nodded. 'I understand. I think that is what I liked and admired in you from the very beginning. Not for what you were — because I didn't know; but for what you could be if you would only give yourself a chance.'

'Well, now I have that chance.' Anton's voice rose with excitement: he leaned forward in his chair, his face intense with emotion. 'My theatrical managers, my agent, my public, my — women friends and all the rest, think I am dead. Let me stay dead to them and begin again with the intention of making something with my life. What harm can it do, John? I'm hurting no one but myself, I promise you.'

'Your family?'

'I have none. And my friends, if such I have,' he said a little bitterly, 'will only miss me temporarily. I am not indispensable, as you pointed out.'

John sighed. 'I have no more arguments. You've already explained about the Englishman who did die yesterday in Castilio of fever and how you will tell the old and rather vacant registrar that a mistake was made in the man's identity, persuading him to alter the name in his register to yours.'

'Of course I shall notify the man's family myself,' Anton added. 'He was travelling alone, so no one knows of the circumstances of his death.'

'Fate seems to have played into your hands,' John commented dryly.

Anton nodded a little wearily. It seemed to him that they were talking in circles, going over and over the same ground. He found it difficult to concentrate on the conversation, for his mind persisted in thinking of Ruth and how she would react to the news of his death. He hoped she would not feel the blow too deeply, but that was thinking along the lines that she still loved him, which he knew was not so. He also hoped that she wouldn't feel a great relief and thankfulness at being rid of her husband so easily. But he rejected this notion: Ruth was too good, too warm-hearted and she had loved him once.

John was speaking again and he suddenly realized that he hadn't heard a word.

' . . . in the country, Cornwall, in fact. It's quiet . . . '

'I'm sorry, John, what were you saying? I was thinking of something else.'

What or who? wondered John, to bring such pain to his friend's eyes. But he only smiled gently and repeated: 'I was saying that once you are back in England you can go to my brother's farm in the country, in Cornwall. It's only a tiny village, but set in beautiful countryside. Adam has a small farm, but it keeps him and my other brother, Luke, busy. Adam would welcome you as a guest for any length of time.'

'That sounds too much of an imposition. Do you realize that I no longer have any money of my own, except what I have in my wallet at the moment?'

'You've been trying to impress that on me all evening. I know you have no money. Adam wouldn't expect money from you, as long as you pulled your weight on the farm — especially this summer. They are always busiest in summer, as Adam shows his cattle at agricultural shows, which means Luke is more often than not alone on the farm and could do with extra help.'

'You mean — work on the farm?'

'That's right. I told you that you'd never known real manual labour. I think it will do you a damn sight more good than night-clubbing, play-acting and women-chasing ever did.'

'It sounds a pleasant prospect,' he commented ironically.

'You could be at home there. You will live as a man should live — work hard, sleep and eat well — all at regular times . . .'

'Doesn't play come into it?'

'Adam and Luke know how to play, when necessary. And when they have the time.' John laughed suddenly at Anton. 'Don't look so anxious. I assure you it isn't as dreadful as it sounds. It may be the back of beyond, but plenty happens there, and my brothers aren't clodhoppers or halfwits.'

'I didn't think they were,' Anton protested quickly, but he was dismayed at the swiftness with which John had read his half-formed thoughts.

'Then you think it a good idea?'

'If I have time to write — do you think the atmosphere would be conducive to writing?' Anton asked, still reluctant to commit himself.

'Time enough for writing when you have found out what life is really like, shorn of all its cheap glamour and gay artificiality. Try living for a time — you'll find the writing will come easily enough later — if you really want to write, you'll find the time. As for atmosphere, there is none at The Haven — not as you know it — only contentment, the quiet joy of a job well done, and healthy tiredness . . . ' he broke off. 'If you feel it will be too countrified for you, after your town life, then say so. I won't force you into anything,' he added with the countryman's reserve, but he waited anxiously for Anton's answer.

'Haven't I said I want a new life? This will be different to anything I've ever experienced; you may not think it, John, but I really prefer the simple things in life. I've often disliked the emptiness one finds in town society, but there just hasn't been the time to find anything else.'

The two men, so alike in looks and build, so totally different in character, sat discussing at greater length the small village of Cuddlesmere and The Haven, John's home. Anton had not known that John was of Cornish stock, but as he listened to him he heard traces of the countryman in his outlook on life, the simple direct approach to every subject, and he admired him. Nostalgia was evident in John's description of his home, and Anton sensed his loneliness, his close kinship with home and family. He asked him why he had ever left Cornwall.

John shrugged. 'I was wild when I was young,' he answered. 'I decided I wasn't cut out for a farmer's life; when I was seventeen I left home for London, after a bitter quarrel with my father. He never forgave me, for I was his favourite son and the hurt went deep. He died a year later, without seeing me again. Adam took over the farm. I grew away from everything I had ever known: like you, I tried a new life, but found, too late, that it was the old life I'd really wanted and still needed.'

'There's no hard feeling between you and your brothers?'

'None at all. Adam and Luke understand that I felt I was entitled to a life of my own. For them Cuddlesmere and the farm was enough. For me it wasn't.'

Anton had never known such interest in other people before and he was surprised at the intensity of feeling with which he listened to John.

'I think there is something *you* need

at The Haven and I hope you find it,'
John added, with a little smile, 'and
find yourself at the same time.'

'How solemn we both are to-night.'
Anton changed the subject, his volatile
personality coming to the fore. 'We
planned such a gay evening.'

'We can have gaiety other nights.
To-night we needed this conversation.'
John rose and poured fresh drinks
for himself and Anton. Handing it
to Anton, he smiled at him. 'Here's
to our friendship.'

'I'm grateful for yours,' Anton replied
warmly. 'I hope I never do anything to
lose it.'

'You never will,' John promised.
There was silence as each man silently
toasted the other.

★ ★ ★

There were no difficulties with regard
to Anton's return to England. John
chartered a private plane and they flew
back to their own country together.

John had already been in touch with his brothers, and without telling them all about Anton, told them enough to make them immediately extend a welcome to the latter to spend as long as he chose at the farm without obligation.

Three weeks after the announcement of Anton Radinov's death in England's newspapers, he entered the white-walled Cornish farmhouse as Anton Marshall, with John close behind him and Adam leading the way.

Adam Newman was a stocky Cornishman, not as tall as John but with sinewy muscles and an earthy grace. Anton had been surprised at the facial resemblance between the two brothers.

Anton had immediately liked the sleepy village with its curving main street, the demure little cottages, the old-fashioned shop; there was a church tucked away behind heavily foliaged green trees and a cemetery with its untidy rows of tombstones; the village boasted two pubs, one, The Green

Man, was quite a modern building and Adam had told him that the place had been built only thirty years ago and was still considered by most of the villagers as 'unfit for human entry', although the publican and his wife were two of the friendliest and most charming people he had met; the other pub, The English Yeoman, was very old, and had raftered ceilings, mullioned windows, and the old men of the village retired there most evenings to play the good old English game of skittles. There was no cinema, no dance-hall; Adam told Anton that the young people had to go into Yalton, the nearest town, which was fourteen miles away, if they wanted to dance or see the latest films.

'But,' Adam added, 'most of our young people are contented enough with the village life, good honest work, a hop once a month in the parish hall, or an occasional bazaar or wedding — they find their entertainment in the simple things.'

Privately Anton thought it all sounded

very dull, and decided he knew no young people who would be content with such a dull existence.

He liked the farmhouse on sight: it had a welcoming, homely look. The long, low room which they entered was very pleasant. The white walls and the heavy oak rafters, chintz curtains at the casement windows, and the comfortable old-fashioned furniture — all were exactly right in such surroundings. Anton looked about him, noticing the spotlessly clean floors and furniture, the gleam of well-polished brass, the sunlight glinting on the shining window-panes Anton wondered if Adam and his brother kept the house so neat and clean, or if there was a woman on the farm.

John sat down in the window-seat and brought out his cigarettes, which he offered first to Anton and then to Adam. Anton accepted, but Adam shook his head, taking his pipe from his pocket.

'I'd rather have this, thanks.' He

took up a box of matches, struck one and held it first to the cigarettes which John and Anton had, and then kindled his pipe.

'What do you think of it?' John asked Anton, who seated himself beside him on the window-seat.

'Delightful.' Anton took a deep breath.

John smiled at his brother, who had glanced up from tamping his pipe to hear Anton's answer. 'You will be happy here,' John said slowly, as he had remarked once before.

'Yes,' Anton agreed. 'I understand what you meant about the lack of atmosphere. There is a sense of timelessness about the house.'

John nodded. 'Exactly. It isn't easy to describe, but I think that's a very good word for it.' He turned to glance through the window. 'Where's Luke, Adam. I want him to meet Anton.'

'He's tending the cattle for me. He'll be in shortly, gasping for tea.' Adam grinned at Anton and explained: 'Farm

273

work is very thirsty work. Luke is a great one for a mug of tea as soon as he comes in, so the kettle is constantly on the boil.'

'What's he like, your brother Luke?' Anton asked curiously. 'Does he resemble you and John?'

'Wait and see!' John said quickly before his brother could reply. Then slowly, he added: 'I hope you and Luke like each other. He's a strange man, unless you understand his ways. Don't be misled by his manner towards people, will you?'

Anton raised enquiring eyebrows.

'Do you mind if I slip out for a few minutes?' Adam interrupted. 'One of my cows is due to calve and I want to see if she's comfortable.'

'Go on, Adam. I'll see that tea is made by the time you get back — and bring Luke with you.' John rose. 'By the way, where's Nancy?'

'Up at the vicarage, nursing old Mrs. Best. She's laid up with arthritis again,' Adam said over his shoulder as he went through the wooden door into the farmyard.

'Nancy?' Anton looked at John.

'Luke's wife. She keeps the place so spotless. They would never have the time to tend the farm and the house as well. She's a good little thing.' John went into the scullery and left Anton alone.

He wandered about the room, running his fingers gently down the brass warming-pans that hung either side of the huge fireplace, wondering how old they were: he noticed how clean and shining they and the brass fire-irons were kept. He idly ran his eyes over the titles of the books in the bookcase and was surprised to find them modern and fairly intellectual. He grinned as he remembered that he had imagined John's brothers to be country bumpkins. Adam was far from being half-witted and Anton felt the same kind of kinship with him that he felt for John and knew that he would find peace and friendship here in this tiny village, so far away from town and society. He went to stand in front of the casement, and watched the rolling pastures, fresh and green, some acres of land, and wondered if they all belonged to Adam. John had told him that Adam concentrated mostly on his cattle and Luke tended the pastures, but that in the harvesting and busy seasons both men worked on the land. Anton felt a stirring of interest as he remembered John's remarks on his younger brother. Thinking of Luke reminded him that he was a married man, that as yet his wife Nancy was but a name and Anton decided she was probably a typical country girl, born in the village and bred to farm life.

John came into the room with a tray on which were laid cups and saucers for him and Anton, mugs for his two brothers, sugar bowl and milk jug. He put the tray down on the refectory table that stood in the centre of the room. He looked so domesticated that Anton was surprised.

'You should get married, John,'

he said suddenly. 'Have you never considered it?'

John glanced up from his task of laying out the crockery. 'I didn't know you were an advocate of marriage!' he said, smiling.

Anton shrugged. 'I'm not really, but it struck me that you're the type who should marry. You might make a comfortable husband for some girl.'

John did not answer for a moment: he poured milk into the cups and carefully measured out sugar into each. Then he came to stand beside Anton and looked through the open window on to the land and the farm buildings.

'Yes,' he admitted. 'I suppose I should marry. But my brother married the only girl I ever cared for.' He said this quietly.

'Nancy?'

'Yes. Nancy.' He drew a long breath and exhaled it in a sigh. 'It's a long story, and the kettle's boiling,' he added with a smile.

'A polite way of saying that you'd

rather I didn't know anything about it?'

'There's really nothing to tell. Nancy preferred Luke to me.' His face closed against further questions, and he changed the subject abruptly. 'What do you think of Adam?'

'I like him,' Anton replied with sincerity. 'I think he's a fine person.'

'Good. I've always thought so. Anyway, I must make the tea. I won't be a minute.' John hastened into the scullery and returned almost instantly with a steaming pot of tea. As he did so, Adam came in from the farmyard.

'Tea ready? Good.'

'Timed very nicely,' John commented, grinning. 'Where's Luke?'

'He won't be long. He's cooling his head under the pump.'

Adam took a mug of tea from his brother and sat down in a comfortable armchair, crossing one knee over the other.

The door swung open and Luke stood in the doorway. Anton turned at the sudden entry. Luke looked curiously at him. Slowly he ran his eyes over the stranger from head to toe, unsmilingly. Anton returned the gaze and both men felt a strong surge of dislike for each other. Anton could not believe that this young man was brother to John and Adam.

Luke Newman was tall, taller than his brother John: he had a crop of jet black curls that glistened wetly now and fell untidily over his brow; he was handsome, with piercing black eyes that looked now like cold black marble as he stared haughtily at Anton. His skin was very dark and only faintly tinged with the ruddiness of his brother's complexion. Working on the land in all weathers had bronzed him, and Anton, studying him, decided that he resembled a Romany in every line of his haughty good looks and carriage. Not only was Luke tall, but he was sinewy, broad-shouldered and muscular: he gave the impression of great strength. As he moved, his muscles rippled: he wore no shirt and his working dungarees clung so tightly to his massive thighs that it seemed they must split at the seams when he walked.

He came in silently, and Anton felt his dominant, virile strength and the hot passionate nature that trembled behind the cold and haughty exterior.

'Anton, my brother Luke,' Adam said coolly.

Luke nodded to the stranger, his face impassive and Anton felt hot blood rise to his cheeks at the countryman's indifference. It was a new experience for him and he smarted under it. Neither Adam nor John seemed to notice that Luke had scarcely been polite to their guest.

John turned to Adam. 'How was the cow?'

'She's fairly comfortable. But I think the calf will come to-night.'

'Which means you'll be up half the night again,' Luke said sharply. His voice was strong, deep and vibrant.

It suddenly occurred to Anton that a voice such as Luke's would rouse an audience to interest and stimulation in a theatre.

'That's right,' Adam agreed mildly, sipping his tea.

'You pamper those cows — like women, they're best left alone when calving.' Luke drank gustily from his mug and placed it when empty on the table. He sat down on the table's edge, his massive arms crossed on his bare chest.

'You don't sound like a farmer, Luke,' Adam replied quietly but with anger behind his voice. 'You know quite well that some cows need more attention than women when they're about to calve. Damson needs me and she's going to have me there to help her, even if I'm up *all* night. As for women — well, you've had no experience of a woman in labour and I have. You don't even know how to treat a pregnant woman,' he added bitterly.

'Leave Nancy out of this. She's all right. If she cries a bit lately, it's because she is pregnant.'

'It couldn't be that she's unhappy?' Adam asked sarcastically.

'Why should she be unhappy?' Luke asked quietly.

'Because you treat her like an animal instead of a woman,' Adam flared, his nostrils quivering with rage and white about the mouth.

'The way I treat my wife is my affair. She married me, not Adam Newman. If she is unhappy, if she has complaints, let her come to me and not snivel on your shoulder.'

'You're not the kind of man a woman would go to in sorrow and pain,' Adam told him slowly. 'I've seen a suffering animal turn from you, Luke, because you don't know how to handle them. That's why you're sensible enough to stick to the land.'

'I'm sure our guest doesn't appreciate our family brawls,' Luke said suddenly.

Adam looked contrite. 'I'm sorry,

Anton. I'm afraid that we're sometimes a little quick-tempered with each other after a day's work on the farm.'

John had paid hardly any attention to his brother's argument. He stood now, looking out at the farmlands, and suddenly he said: 'Here's Nancy now.'

Anton followed his glance and watched the girl, clumsily pregnant, who came up the path towards the farmhouse. A pain gripped suddenly at his heart, for there was something about her, an air of vulnerability, that reminded him vividly of Ruth. Oh, God, he thought, if I am to think of Ruth every time I look at this woman, then I cannot stay here.

Nancy was young and fair and pretty, though she looked wan and tired now in the heat of the afternoon. She caught her lips between her teeth as a slight pain stabbed her side. She had hurried from the village — hurried to get back to Luke — hurried towards the house where she was at once so happy and yet so sad. She threw an anxious glance at the farm buildings, seeking for her husband, and then looked towards the house.

Adam flung open the door and went to meet her. Anton watched the tenderness with which he took her basket from her and slipped an arm about her waist, talking to her gently. Anton glanced at Luke and surprised a look of intense possessiveness as he watched his wife and brother together. It was not a loving look, but more one of pride in possession.

Adam and Nancy entered the house and she smiled breathlessly at John and Anton before turning towards Luke. She smiled tremulously at him, her heart in her eyes. He ran his eyes over her swollen body and flushed face, unkempt hair, and turned away. Anton was shocked at the contemptuous gesture. Nancy stared at Luke, longing for a smile, a word of affection from him, some gesture to show that she meant something to him, but none came and she too turned away, pain in her eyes that did not mirror to the full the depth of pain in her heart. She knew that Luke had never loved her. He thought of her in the same way as he thought of his dog, Clem. She was a possession, something that was really his and which nothing could take away. When he was in the mood, Luke would be affectionate towards Clem, running his hands over his body, fondling his ears, teasing him gently: at another time he would throw him a word or a hasty caress, perhaps ignore him altogether; and so he treated his wife, in the same careless, indifferent way.

Nancy sighed and glanced at John. Her eyes softened and she smiled. 'It's so nice to see you again. You look so well.'

John went to her and kissed her soft cheek. 'You're looking tired. You've been hurrying, too. Surely that isn't good for you.'

'I knew you would be here. I wanted to see you,' she said shyly.

'Well, come and meet Anton.' John drew her over to his friend. Anton rose and greeted her warmly. She smiled at him and he was struck again by the sensitive eyes, the air of vulnerability. She was like a child suddenly grown up and wishing she could be a child again. Anton's eyes were tender as he looked down at her. She was so young, he thought, too young to be the wife of a man like Luke, who carelessly hurt her and would go on hurting her throughout their life together. Anton had noticed the way she had turned to her husband and her deep love for him had been written all over her face. She should hide her emotions, he thought suddenly: hide behind a veneer, a façade, so that she wouldn't be so easily hurt.

As they stood together, chatting about the journey, Nancy suddenly put her hand to her side as the former pain stabbed her anew. Adam noticed immediately and went to her anxiously.

'Sit down, Nancy. You're a silly girl to rush from the village like that.'

'Yes, I know.' She smiled wanly.

'How is Mrs. Best?' Adam asked, as he led her to the armchair he had recently vacated. He fussed about her, pouring her tea, making her comfortable.

'She's a little better to-day,' Nancy replied. 'She has such faith in Dr. Kershaw, but we all know that nothing can be done.' She sighed.

'Well, you should be more careful, or you'll be the one in bed and we'll have old Mrs. Best tottering up here on her sticks to nurse you,' John said gaily.

Luke followed the conversation, his eyes sombre and withdrawn. 'Stop fussing,' he said sharply to Adam. 'You'll make Nancy think she's an invalid, instead of a normal woman having a normal pregnancy.'

Adam turned on him angrily: 'Normal this time, thank God, but *I* don't forget so easily that Nancy has already lost one child.'

Luke had the grace to flush. He turned to his wife. 'Are you tired?'

'No, not really,' she lied, her small hand going quickly to touch his with a fluttering, appealing gesture. Luke nodded and strode to the door, the sunlight catching his wet curls. 'Luke, you've had your head under the pump,' Nancy added with a tender smile. He made no answer and left the house, striding towards the barn. Nancy rose and without any explanation ran after him. Luke turned to wait for her as she called his name and then they walked on together, his arm slipped about her waist.

12

Anton soon settled in at The Haven. A few days after their arrival, John returned to Spain

Anton found a great deal to interest him about the farm and the house. As yet, he did not help the brothers in their work — that would come later. He found himself thinking constantly about the three people he was living with. Luke he could not fathom: he was saturnine and kept up his attitude of indifference towards Anton. Sometimes Anton thought wryly that Luke seemed hardly aware of his presence. Nancy he found endearing: he was sorry for her, and yet knew she would resent his pity. At times he wanted to thrash Luke for the way he would speak to his wife, but he knew it was none of his business. Adam was his friend: they found a great deal in common, and Anton often sought him out during the day to talk to him, to learn about the farm and the animals that Adam loved with an all-absorbing passion.

One day Anton stood talking to Adam while he gently tended the new calf and her mother, the sorrowful-eyed Damson.

That morning Luke had scolded Nancy for resting when she should have been busy about the house. He seemed to think that she should be as stoic as an animal and never give way to tiredness or pain, both of which were natural at this stage of her pregnancy. Anton had been reading a book, seated on the doorstep of the back door, clad in grey slacks and soft white shirt. As usual, Luke had ignored him.

Nancy had listened to Luke's terse comments quietly, and then had risen from the armchair to go about her work. Luke caught her by the arm.

'Why are you so sullen? Aren't you happy?'

'Of course I am, Luke.'

She looked up at him trustingly, her love in her eyes, and his lip curled as he studied her wan face, the blue eyes so large in their loving expression.

'One day you'll find the courage to tell the truth,' he sneered. She coloured: he was right; she was afraid, constantly afraid of losing him or of angering him. She always said what she thought he wanted to hear.

Now she replied: 'I don't understand you.'

He laughed curtly. 'That's the trouble.' He turned away and she put out a timid hand to touch his sleeve. Instinctively he recoiled from her touch: but he gazed down at her with a strange expression in his dark eyes, and a moment later he raised his hand to brush a lock of hair from her face with a rough caress. Tears came into her eyes. He bent his head to brush his lips across her mouth, then strode from the room, an enigmatic smile curving his mouth.

Remembering now, Anton said to

Adam: 'Why the hell does Nancy stand for the way Luke is to her?'

Adam shrugged. 'She loves him. How can you explain why a woman does anything when she's in love. She sees no wrong in him, no matter how he hurts her. She can explain away his every word and gesture satisfactorily. She would tell you it is only his way, that every man is different to another.'

'He is so strange. So — withdrawn, so completely self-sufficient. He acts as if he needs no one and nothing. I should hate to know he was my enemy.'

'Luke is incapable of hate,' Adam said slowly. 'He can only feel indifference, which is worse. He was a strange child, full of tense emotions — he would guard with his life the oddest things, yet he had so little to call his own, as the youngest son. No one had time to try to understand him, and he rebuffed anyone who did try, anyway.'

Anton nodded. 'He's very interesting,

anyway. Like a problem that nags at you until it is solved.'

Adam did not answer for a moment, as he gently rubbed the calf's ears and stroked his nose tenderly.

'Do you mean to try to solve Luke?' he asked finally. 'It will be a difficult problem.'

'I mean to help Nancy,' Anton retorted strongly.

'She might resent your help.'

'You may be right, but I intend to try.' He paused, looked at Adam and then continued: 'I shall always be glad I came to Cuddlesmere, Adam. For the first time in my life I am concerned with other people and their problems, instead of my own.'

Adam nodded. 'What shall I call this calf?' he asked idly, but Anton knew that he had listened intently to his remarks and approved them.

He made a non-committal reply, and after a few more minutes left Adam; remembering a message he had undertaken to deliver for Nancy, he turned his footsteps towards the village. He strode along, whistling softly to himself, feeling contentment pervade his being as he looked about him — at the blue of the clear sky, the proud beauty of the trees with their foliage turned heavenwards in green wonder, the rolling farmland around him: to his right a herd of sheep, a few grazing and some lying supine in the sun; to his left the fine herd of cattle that was Adam's pride and joy. As always, his active mind was busy — with thoughts of the Newman family, Nancy and her coming child. He wondered what effect his child would have on Luke; would it help to soften that grim exterior, would it coax a smile, laughter or gentle words from the Cornishman. Anton thought it unlikely. He recalled Nancy's pure sweet face and the clumsy grace of her large body, a soft tenderness curving his lips. He sighed; as always, the thought of Luke's wife brought him memories of Ruth. He missed her with a constant ache of longing; he missed the love she once had felt for him and had never failed to show. His arms ached to embrace her and his lips missed the sweet coolness of her kiss. She had been his most precious possession in life — and he himself had thrown her away, turned her out of his life, denied himself an existence so that she should find happiness without him.

Was she with Gregg? Was that where her happiness lay? he wondered. Did Gregg now know the joy of her lips on his, the wonder of her love? Thoughts of his wife, his love, in the arms of his best friend were torture to Anton, but he could not stop himself thinking them, again and again. Not only during the sunlit hours, when he strolled the Cornish lanes or talked with Nancy in the cool farmhouse or watched Adam tending his cattle, but in the darkness of the night when he lay sleepless, his arms empty and his whole being hungry for the love of the girl he had once called 'wife'.

★ ★ ★

Had he but known, Ruth was far from being happily embraced by Gregg. She could never put the thought of Anton out of her mind, nor could her love for him lessen in any measure. It was five weeks since she had lost her husband, yet the sharp ache of loss remained with her. All of Gregg's kind attentions, his consideration for her, could not stave off her longing for Anton, though she appreciated all he did for her.

Even as Anton strolled down the lanes of Cuddlesmere, thinking of his wife, she sat in the garden of her parents' home in Sussex, needlework idle in her hands, her expression sad as she recalled her life with Anton.

Gregg was ostensibly reading a newspaper as he sat in the deck-chair beside her, but he was aware of her silent preoccupation and her idle hands. He glanced covertly at her face and longed to kiss away its sadness.

He thought of how deeply Anton's death had affected her; how ill she had been for a while with the reaction to the shock. It had been feared for a few days that she would lose her child and Gregg knew that such a loss would have broken her heart completely. Ruth felt that Anton's son was the only consolation she had in life and she waited and planned for his birth with an intense longing.

Ruth's mother had come to London directly she had read in the newspapers of her daughter's loss. The news that Ruth was married — in such secrecy — had hurt her, but Mrs. Strong had shown nothing of this, but was by her daughter's side in the minimum of time, to comfort her and help her and, when she discovered her illness, to nurse her back to health. When Ruth was well enough to travel, she returned to Latimer with her mother, although insisting that her son be born in London and determined that she would make arrangements for this event. Ruth was sure that if Anton had known of the existence of his son he would have chosen London, the cosmopolitan city that he loved so much, for his birthplace.

Gregg knew that although Anton had hurt Ruth so badly, she had forgiven him without reserve: she always blamed herself for the break-up of their marriage; she had never been a good enough wife to him, she had doubted his loyalty to her and had done all the wrong things — enough to drive him away from her.

Ruth only regretted that she had never known Anton's love, for she felt that he had been a man who could know great depth of feeling if only he had allowed himself the luxury of loving. Ruth told herself that his natural reserve had held him back, a reserve that no other person had ever sensed in him; that he had been too used to consider only himself to suddenly alter his whole mode of living — she found all manner of excuses for Anton's behaviour and so gradually erased any feeling of resentment at his treatment of her that she might ever have had.

Gregg loved her even more since Anton's death: he had admired her for her courage, her bearing and her spirit. Even while she carried another man's child, he found her desirable and longed to marry her. But he knew it was much too soon. He believed that the mental process she was going through with regard to Anton and his way of living would eventually alter her concept of her husband out of all recognition; he believed that then she would be ready to love again — and Gregg thought himself prepared to wait until then.

Ruth sensed the way Gregg felt about her and she was sorry that she had to hurt him: she knew that she would never marry again. Her son would, in a small measure, take Anton's place in her life. She counted the days until December, when he would be born.

The time dragged interminably — it was only the third week in July; five months yet before she could hold her child in her arms.

She sighed.

'Ruth, you're tired. Would you like to go in?'

She shook her head. 'No. I'm all right. I like to sit out here in the sun.' A thought struck her and she laid her hand on his arm. 'You're not bored, Gregg? I mean, bored with the country, stuck down here with me?'

'No, or course not. I could go back to London if I wanted to, you know.' He smiled. 'Who could be bored with you?'

'Anton used to be, I think,' she replied softly. 'That's probably why he went out so much. I was so different to all his friends — and he liked a gay life.'

'He married you because you were different,' Gregg replied swiftly.

She hesitated a moment, then said: 'Did Anton ever tell you why he did

300

marry me, Gregg?'

Gregg studied his cigarette intently. 'We talked about it, yes. Before you were married. Afterwards he never discussed you with me. He told me that you were the only woman he could ever imagine as a wife. I think he was pretty fond of you.' Gregg could not bring himself to lie about Anton's feelings for Ruth. He knew that Ruth longed to hear that Anton had loved her so much that he couldn't face life without her, although Gregg sensed that she herself knew it had not been so.

Ruth made no reply, but after a moment or two she picked up her needlework and began to sew.

'You've been wonderful to me, Gregg,' she said presently. 'No girl could have a better friend. Since the first day we met you've always been kind and considerate, always there to cheer me up and make me laugh when I've felt depressed, by my side as soon as you knew Anton was dead. I don't deserve such friendship.'

'Oh, nonsense!' Gregg laughed, colouring. 'You forget Anton was my best friend, and I thought the world of him. It was only natural that I should extend my friendship to his wife and, in any case, without that qualification, I'm very fond of you, Ruth. You know that. I'd do anything for you.'

She smiled, looking into his eyes, that radiated warmth and affection, a constancy of feeling that made her feel safe, protected and inexplicably cheered.

'I feel guilty,' she said with a smile. 'While you're with me you have no time for any other interests; I am taking you away from all your friends.'

'Maybe, but I'm happy with you, Ruth. I don't need anyone else.'

'Oh — but surely — you must have women friends. Don't you miss them? Isn't there a girl you prefer to be with above all others? Someone you might marry one day?'

'Yes . . . ' he replied slowly. 'There is a girl. A wonderful girl — but I'm not very hopeful about marrying her.'

'What a shame, Gregg. You deserve to be happy — to be married to the girl you love!'

'There's nothing I want more.'

'Why aren't you with her? You don't have to worry about me, Gregg dear. I'm all right now. I wish you would go back to town and be happy.' She impressed on him anxiously. 'I've been so selfish, keeping you to myself.'

Gregg smiled into her anxious face. 'I'm teasing you, Ruth. Don't worry.'

She looked puzzled. 'Then there isn't a girl?'

'Oh, yes. There certainly is — but I don't have to go to town to be with her.' He laid his hand over hers with a sudden warm pressure. 'I'm sorry, Ruth. I didn't mean to tell you for months yet, but it must be more and more obvious every day that I love you.'

'Me?' Ruth was astonished.

'Yes, you, my darling. I've always loved you, Ruth. I always will. But if you are unhappy about it, then I won't mention it again until I think you want to hear it.'

'Oh, Gregg!' she said in distress. 'I had no idea. I know you were fond of me — but I never thought — I mean . . . ' She trailed off, her lovely grey eyes downcast.

He lifted her hand to his lips. 'I know what you mean, my dear. I know it's too soon, and I'm sorry. But I'd like you to think about me one day as a possible husband. Your son will need a father, you know, and I happen to be very fond of children — so if you marry me for no other reason, then I shall be happy. You see, darling, your happiness is the only thing that concerns me. It's always been like that. I loved you from the day I met you and it almost cost me my friendship with Anton, because I couldn't reconcile myself completely to the fact that you were his wife.'

'Please, Gregg — don't!' Ruth exclaimed, sudden tears springing to her eyes.

In an instant Gregg had her in his arms, her head on his shoulder. 'I'm sorry, my darling, truly sorry. I was thinking only of myself, but I didn't mean to distress you.'

'Dear Gregg.' she murmured. 'You so rarely think of yourself — you put me first every time and it's so unfair. You're much too good to me and I love you for it — but not in the way you want to be loved.'

'Maybe it will come,' he said against her hair. 'I'll wait — and hope. Meanwhile, I'll be Good Old Gregg, ever faithful and always there when you want him. And,' he smiled, 'sometimes there when you don't.'

Ruth smiled through her tears, and brushed her lashes with the back of her hand.

Gregg was true to his word. Never again in the following months did he mention his love for her to Ruth. But it was apparent now in his care of her, his kindness and loving consideration, that he tried to be brotherly but just failed. Ruth was relying more and more on him, and when he returned to London, as he did quite frequently, she missed him. In September he had to leave Latimer for town, for the opening of the new play which Anton had been originally chosen to act in: Flavek had approached Gregg to see if he would take over the part and he had agreed. There was a period of intensive rehearsals a fortnight before the opening night and it finally began the first week in October. It was a great success, and Gregg, who had been well up the ladder anyway for some time past, found himself a little more in the limelight and a lot more in demand, so he had very little time to spend with Ruth.

She had made arrangements to return to the town flat at the end of October, and then to go into a nursing home to have the baby in mid-December. Mrs. Strong did not want Ruth to return alone to London in such an advanced state of pregnancy, but her daughter insisted that she was well able to take care of herself. She was so insistent that, wisely, nothing more was said.

★ ★ ★

Jay and Rona attended the opening night of *Fools In Heaven*, in which Gregg played the lead; after the show they went on to the party which was thrown by Sol Flavek.

They were still engaged, on the platonic basis, and to all appearances very happy. Rona had settled down and lost some of her flightiness. Jay was as cynical as ever, but excellent company. They attended a great many opening nights, parties and night-clubs, and had a lot of gay friends, all of which appealed to Rona's love of a good time.

Jay supplied Rona with a drink then strolled over to speak to Gregg, leaving her with a couple of admirers.

Flushed with success, Gregg greeted him warmly. 'Jay, old man!' They shook hands. 'I'm glad you could come along. Have a drink?'

Jay indicated the glass in his hand. 'I'm happy for the moment, thanks. Congratulations, I thoroughly enjoyed the show — without reservation!'

Gregg grinned. 'Good write-up tomorrow?'

'You can bank on it. You've got a winner on your hands — and I'll guarantee you steady employment for the next two years, at least.'

'I'm glad to hear it. That's always appreciated in this profession,' Gregg told him, smiling.

Jay offered him a cigar. 'I don't think I've seen you since Anton Radinov died, have I?' He shook his head. 'A great loss.'

Gregg's face clouded at mention of his friend. He took a cigar with a murmured word of thanks, and said: 'I think everyone in the theatre must miss him. One doesn't find geniuses every day.' He paused, and added: 'By the way, I still have to congratulate you on your engagement to Rona.'

'I hope you aren't saying that with your tongue in your cheek,' Jay answered lightly.

'No. I really mean it. I think you are probably just the man to tame Rona.'

'She needs taming,' Jay agreed with a smile. 'But I'm enjoying the task. Underneath all that superficiality, she's quite a sweet girl.' He glanced across at Rona, as she stood in a circle of men friends. 'Her trouble is that she's had too much of that sort of thing.' He nodded in Rona's direction and Gregg smiled, secretly in agreement. Jay turned back to him. 'How's Anton's wife these days? Has she had her baby yet?'

'Not till December. She's very well and just about getting over the shock of losing Anton. She was really devoted to him, you know.'

'I thought she was a very sweet little thing, when I met her. I'm really not surprised that Anton snapped her up, the sly dog.' He drained his glass. 'So you're looking after her welfare these days?'

Gregg gave him a quick look. 'Don't try to make anything of it. We're just good friends and nothing more. Anton was my best friend, remember.'

'Of course, I realize that,' Jay hastened to assure him, and decided to change the subject. Gregg was obviously sensitive about Anton Radinov's widow, a sure sign of attachment of some sort. 'By the way, Gregg, did you hear that I've been asked to compère a record programme on television? My agent fixed it and it's a plum of a contract. It's due to start in the New Year.'

'Congratulations. I hope it's a successful venture. What does Rona think about it?'

'She's very pleased.'

'When do you and Rona plan to be married?' Gregg asked idly. Jay shrugged.

'That's up to Rona to decide.' Conversation turned to Rona, and from her they went on to discuss theatrical news.

Rona was kept busy talking to various friends, but she frequently glanced towards Jay as he chatted with Gregg. It was perfectly usual for Jay to wander off at parties and leave her to fend for herself, and Rona normally was quite contented to be the centre of a crowd of admiring men, who were delighted to wait on her every whim. But to-night she felt at a loss and wished that Jay had stayed with her. She excused herself from her friends and strolled across to join Gregg and Jay.

They turned to greet her.

'Hallo, Rona. How are you?'

'I'm very well, Gregg. How's yourself? I hear you've been buried in the country for the last few months.'

He nodded. 'And enjoying it. I prefer the country to town. May I wish you every happiness on your engagement, Rona?'

'Thank you.' Faced with Anton's best friend and remembering the circumstances of her engagement, she flushed.

'Will you excuse me?' Gregg said. 'There's someone I want to talk to.' With a curtness that was foreign to him, he nodded to Rona and walked away.

Rona looked after him. 'Well,' she said, 'that was a neat exit. I guess he didn't like my company.'

'Don't be so sensitive. Naturally, there are other people here he wants to have a word with.'

'And I should be grateful for those few words?' she snapped.

He looked at her sharply. 'I guess you want another drink to sweeten you a little.'

'I don't want a drink. I want to go home.'

He shrugged. 'Very well. I'll take you home.' Women were illogical, he considered, as they made their farewells — they insisted on going to parties, but as soon as they arrived they insisted on leaving. It was obvious that meeting

Gregg had upset Rona: perhaps he had reminded her too forcibly of Anton Radinov. With a sudden sense of depression, Jay wondered if Rona had felt the loss of her lover more keenly than she had shown. He drove her to her flat in silence. She sat beside him, gazing through the side window on to the empty London streets, her face turned away from him.

When they arrived at her address he pulled up and waited for her to speak.

'Are you coming in?' she asked coldly.

'How can I refuse such a charming invitation,' he mocked. 'Yes, I'm coming in, if only for a drink, seeing that we left the party before I'd had barely a glass in my hand.'

Léonie hurried to the door at the sound of the key in the lock. Rona slipped out of her furs, threw them into her maid's arms, and dismissed her curtly, telling her not to wait up. Jay followed his fiancée into the lounge.

She sat down, slipped off her high-heeled shoes and helped herself to a cigarette from the box on the table in front of her. Jay strolled across to the cabinet and poured himself a drink.

'Do you want one?'

She shook her head. He shrugged, tossed back the drink and poured himself a further glass. Then he walked over to the window and stood looking down into the lighted street below.

Rona stubbed her cigarette after a moment or two, sat with her head bowed and hands clenched. She was torn between two courses of action, yet she knew that she could only take one path and must do so now.

Suddenly she spoke, her voice harsh. 'I can't go on.'

Jay turned. 'What?'

'I can't go on, Jay. I've had enough.'

'Enough of what?' He was surprised at her tone. She was more distressed that he had imagined, but what had upset her he had no idea. He went to her side, put the glass on the table and sat down on the settee beside her. 'What's the matter, Rona?'

'I'm breaking our engagement. I'm giving you the ring back.' She pulled the beautiful solitaire from her finger and placed it quietly on the table.

Jay shrugged. 'Very well. That was our arrangement. When it became inconvenient, we should end it. Or else on mutual agreement.'

'Yes, it's been nothing but a farce from the beginning,' Rona said bitterly.

'That was the way you wanted it,' Jay retorted in amazement.

'I know. But I didn't think — ' She stopped and brushed her beautiful hair back from her face with a weary gesture.

'You didn't think what?' Jay asked with an odd inflection in his voice.

'I didn't think I was going to fall in love with you,' she replied.

'That must have shaken you to the depths!' he commented. If he had been less surprised he would have stopped to think of a suitable answer, but he could hardly believe his ears at Rona's admission.

'You don't believe me,' she stated dully. 'I'm not surprised.'

'How can you expect me to believe it? I'm convinced you don't know the meaning of the word. Nothing in your past life points to it.'

'How I hate your cynicism,' she said quietly. 'I should have known better than to tell you. It would have been much easier to break the engagement and part amicably, under the terms of the agreement.' There was such bitterness in her voice as she said the last phrase that Jay was touched against his will.

'You're really serious, aren't you?'

'Of course I am. I've never been more serious in my life. Don't think I wanted to love you, Jay — not after the things I said when we were first engaged — and not you, because I don't think I even like you very much as a man.'

He grinned. 'Thank you. I appreciate that sentiment. It must be difficult loving a man you don't even like.'

She tried to suppress a smile, but Rona could not be depressed for long. Jay put an arm about her shoulders.

'That's more like you, Rona. I hate to see you unhappy, you know.'

'Do you?'

'Of course. I've grown very fond of you lately. I never knew you could be such a nice person when you liked.' He pressed his lips to her forehead. 'So we can consider ourselves un-engaged, huh? You've called it off, properly?'

'I think so, Jay. I really can't continue like this. It's all so artificial.'

'You're quite sure about this. You want to finish the contract, end the agreement, Rona?'

She nodded. 'Yes, I do.'

'Good.'

Her heart sank. So he was glad, in fact relieved: she wondered unhappily why he had never called it off himself, if that's how he felt.

'Now I can ask you to marry me, without any artificial reasons,' he said.

She looked up at him, eyes suddenly bright. 'Oh, Jay, do you mean it? For God's sake, don't tease me.'

'I'm not teasing,' he said gently. He took her into his arms and held her close. 'I've been waiting for you to break that stupid engagement, so I could ask you to marry me. I would never have married you under the existing arrangement — why, I was almost talked into it. This time I can decide for myself.'

'Do you love me then, Jay?'

'No, of course not.' He laughed. 'I just want to marry the one woman in the world I can fight with one moment and want to kiss the next. They'll call us Mr. and Mrs. Kiss-and-Scratch, my darling, but we'll be happier than most.'

He kissed her and left her breathless and flushed, her eyes sparkling.

Hours later they were still making

plans for their quick marriage and a honeymoon abroad.

Sitting in the circle of his arms, his head against her hair Rona had never been happier.

She smiled, thinking of her affection for Anton in the past, and wondered how she had ever imagined that she loved him. Until this love for Jay had come into her life, she had never really known such a devastating emotion.

She turned her head to kiss the corner of his mouth, and then his lips.

'Darling, do I need to tell you anything about Anton?' she whispered against his lips.

He shook his head. 'I can guess all I need to know, Rona. Anton had a reputation — and you're such a wild, reckless creature. Don't think about the past, darling. The future is all we are concerned with now.'

'The future — with you — will be wonderful, Jay.'

She sounded so happy and her eyes

shone with such radiance that Jay caught her to him suddenly, love surging through him.

In his opinion, everything was working out for the best.

13

Simon Radinov was born on Christmas Eve. Ruth was delighted with her son. She had never doubted that her child would be a boy, but everyone else had feared a disappointment was quite possible.

Gregg visited her at the expensive nursing home the following day, his arms full of presents for her and the baby.

Ruth greeted him warmly, looking radiant. Gregg thought he had never seen her look so lovely and decided that motherhood was the one thing to make any woman complete.

'Have you seen him, Gregg?' she asked eagerly, almost as soon as he arrived. 'He's beautiful!'

Gregg nodded, smiling. 'If he's the one with a mass of black hair and a loud cry, then I saw him. You know, they only let me look through a glass window — and he could have been any of the mites, for all I knew, until he was held up for me by the nurse.'

'He's got Anton's hair without a doubt,' Ruth said, smiling happily. 'But my eyes. Have you ever heard of a black-haired boy with grey eyes, Gregg? It's such an odd combination!'

'You look very well, anyway, Ruth. Lovelier than ever.'

She smiled at the compliment. 'I feel well. And very happy. I'm so pleased he's a boy.'

'What would you have done if he'd been a girl? Sent her back?' Gregg asked laughing, as he sat down beside her bed. It was a large, luxurious room, the best that money could buy. Gregg had insisted on that.

Ruth did not reply for a moment. Then her innate honesty came to the fore and she said: 'I think I would have been very disappointed. But only at first. I should love any child of Anton's, you know that, Gregg.' He nodded. Ruth picked up the bouquet he had laid on the bed and buried her nose in the sweet-smelling flowers. 'These are lovely, Gregg, thank you.'

Gregg took out his cigarette-case and helped himself. He flicked his lighter into life and said casually: 'By the way, I've some news for you.'

'Oh, what? Tell me!' she exclaimed with childlike eagerness.

'Rona and Jay were married yesterday at Caxton Hall,' he answered and smiled widely at her reaction.

'Rona and Jay!' she exclaimed. 'Surely not!' She searched his face, smiling. 'Is it true?'

'Yes, it's true enough.'

'But — we thought . . .'

'It's the last thing we thought would come of their engagement,' he finished for her. 'I guess Jay simply kept Rona on a tight rein and she happened to like it. Anyway, they're married.'

'I am pleased. I hope they'll be really happy,' Ruth said with sincerity.

A few weeks later, Ruth was living again at the flat which she had shared with Anton, her baby son thriving on the loving care which she gave him. It seemed to Ruth that Simon grew daily more like his father: she fancied she could trace the curve of the determined chin, see the arrogance in the child's expression and she studied him eagerly for signs of Anton's sensitive, artistic nature. Gregg laughed at her gently, but understood. He reminded her frequently that Simon was much too young to resemble anyone, but she would not agree.

She was surprised when Rona telephoned her a few days after her return to the flat to ask if she and Jay could come along to see her son. Taken aback, she had the presence of mind to issue a swift and warm invitation.

It was natural that Ruth should feel a surge of resentment against Rona, but as she replaced the receiver and turned to gaze down at her son's innocent and lovely face, her resentment died.

'After all, Simon,' she said to him gently, 'I have you. She has nothing to remind her of Anton. I *am* glad that she has found consolation with Jay and if she's happy, then how can I bear a grudge for something that happened so long ago.'

When they arrived, Ruth felt a little shy, but Jay soon put her at her ease. Rona had the grace to feel a little uncomfortable, but as nothing Ruth said or did served to remind her of the damage she had done the other woman, very soon they were chatting of Simon and his progress like old friends.

Rona was beautiful, as radiant as a bride should be. She was obviously very happy. They had just returned from a touring honeymoon in Europe, which had to be cut short so that Jay could begin his television series. But they planned a trip abroad in six months' time and Rona talked excitedly of the prospect.

They stayed for over an hour and were just about to leave when Gregg arrived. He could not believe his eyes to see Rona and Ruth together, in the same room, and obviously in a harmonious atmosphere.

'What are you two doing here?' he exclaimed, and added quickly: 'I thought you were on honeymoon.'

Jay explained.

'They've brought Simon some lovely presents,' Ruth said happily. 'He's going to be terribly spoilt.'

'I've never seen a lovelier baby,' Rona said.

Gregg grinned, wondering how much Rona knew about children! Rona met his eyes and, being suddenly conscious of his thoughts, shook her head warningly.

'Well, marriage certainly appears to agree with you, Rona.' Gregg was more inclined to be friendly now that Ruth seemed to accept Rona's presence in her home as almost matter of course. He inwardly wondered at Rona, whom it would seem stopped at nothing, and was not in the least perturbed that the husband of the girl she visited had once been her lover.

'I'm enjoying it,' Rona admitted. 'Maybe because it's the first time in my life I can't have my own way all the time.' She laughed huskily. 'I'm lucky if I have a say in anything at all, these days.'

'You're thriving on it, nevertheless,' Jay said with a smile. He was proud of Rona: she had changed in many ways from the thoughtless, proud woman she had been.

'We were just leaving,' Rona told Gregg. 'You and Ruth must come to dinner with us one evening.' She looked from Gregg to her husband. 'You two fix it up between you.'

'It's a little difficult,' Ruth protested. 'Simon is much too young to be left on his own.'

'I'd forgotten him for the moment. Never mind, Ruth. Perhaps when he's a little older . . . '

They left it at that for the time being, and Jay and Rona took their leave.

Gregg turned to Ruth and smiled. 'Well, well, that was a surprise, wasn't it?'

She nodded. 'Yes, it was. But she looks so happy and was so interested in Simon that within minutes I almost forgot what she once was.'

'You mean that she was once Anton's mistress? I'm glad to see that you've at last decided to recognize that fact, Ruth.'

'Don't misunderstand me, Gregg!' she exclaimed. 'I may admit that it was true, but that certainly doesn't blacken Anton in my eyes. I am only sorry that I was such an unsatisfactory wife he had to continue his association with Rona.'

Gregg turned away, a little impatient. 'There are none so blind as those who can't see,' he quoted, and then laughed. 'You'll never change, will you, Ruth? You see life through rose-coloured spectacles and you mean to go on like that.'

'Why shouldn't it be really as lovely as I think it is?'

'Life, you mean? Because, my sweet, it never is. But if being Anton's wife couldn't disillusion you, then I'm certainly not going to try.' He gestured towards Simon as he lay asleep in his cot, which could be seen through the open door of the bedroom. 'I hope you're going to bring your son up with a more practical outlook on life. I think the boy needs a father,' and his heart was in his eyes and voice.

'Please, Gregg!' she pleaded quickly.

'I know. Don't worry, Ruth. I don't mean to pester you with proposals — but I would like you to keep me in mind.'

She nodded, trying to keep her voice light: 'I will. Now, will you have a drink?'

She steered clear of the dangerous subject for the rest of the time he spent with her that evening, but she knew that one day he would not be brushed aside lightly, one day he would demand an answer.

Alone in her room that night, she sighed. Alone but for Simon, innocently asleep in his tiny bed, she longed for company, longed for the warmth and security of male companionship, longed for Anton and the happiness they might have known together.

'What shall I do, Simon?' she whispered to her sleeping son, standing by his cot. Gently she tucked the covers more snugly about his small, sweet body. 'Gregg is so good to me,' she went on aloud. 'So very good — he loves me and he wants to make me happy. If there had never been Anton I could be contented with what Gregg offers me. He would make a good husband, kind and considerate, a loving father too — and you will need a father, Simon my darling. No matter how I try, I can never be both mother and father to you.' She knelt down suddenly beside his cot, and hot tears came swiftly to scald her cheeks. No words could have expressed how deeply she felt the loss of Anton at that moment, how bitter she was that her happiness had been taken away from her.

'If he had known about you, Simon, he would have come back to me, I know,' she sobbed. 'We would have had a second chance of happiness — and I know one day I would have won his love . . .'

The child, as though conscious of the tumult about him, stirred and whimpered in his sleep. His cry penetrated Ruth's unhappiness of spirit and she choked back her tears, patting her baby's shoulder gently. 'There, there, darling,' she crooned. 'It's all right. Go back to sleep.'

She rose and went to the dressing-table. She peered into the mirror in the dim, shaded light and brushed her hair back from her brow. The months of unhappiness had left their mark: she was no longer the sunny girl that loved and laughed and married Anton Radinov, but a mature woman with a look of suffering in her deep grey eyes, a sad lilt to her pretty mouth and a paleness in her cheeks.

'You look old and haggard,' she said to her reflection bitterly. 'Anton wouldn't know you if he were alive and could see you now.' But, her mind argued, if he were alive she wouldn't look like this.

She remembered Rona, beautiful and elegant, charming and sophisticated, eyes less hard now that she had found happiness and love, her whole nature softened by the radiance of her marriage.

But once again, Ruth found solace in thinking that she could not envy Rona while she had Simon, a legacy of her love for Anton and her greatest comfort.

Meanwhile, Ruth was the subject of a conversation that was taking place between Jay and Rona.

* * *

Rona sat at her dressing-table, idly brushing her lovely auburn hair that still fell almost to her waist. Jay had told her it would be sacrilege to have it cut, although it was more fashionable at the moment to wear a short style. Through the open door of the bedroom, which adjoined the lounge of their flat, came the strains of the piano, as Jay picked out melodies, almost unconsciously. He would never play as well as his wife, but he had an attractive touch. An occasional wrong note brought a tender smile to the corners of Rona's mouth. She was thinking of Ruth.

'Darling, do you think Ruth looked sad to-night?' she called. The music stopped and a few moments later Jay came to the doorway. He lounged against the jamb, watching Rona ply her brush with little or no industry.

'Wouldn't you look sad if you lost me?' he countered. He came to her side, swiftly, and took the brush from her hand. 'Let me do this, darling. You're not really concentrating on it.'

'I know,' she said absentmindedly and smiled up at him. 'I'm thinking about Ruth. I wish there was something we could do to make her happier.'

'You could have done something once — it's too late now,' he said with meaning.

'Jay, please don't keep throwing Anton in my face,' she pleaded, laying her hand on his arm. 'Can't you see that I want to put it all behind me. It's in the past — I'm a different woman now. Besides, you hurt me when you say things like that.'

He bent to press a swift kiss on her forehead. 'I'm sorry, darling. I'm a beast to you, sometimes, aren't I?' he said contritely.

'You're forgiven. Anyway, we were talking of Ruth.' She paused. 'Do you really think she is unhappy because of Anton's death? It's so long ago now — over six months, and she has Simon to take his place.'

'You're talking nonsense. When has a child ever taken the place of a man's warm, pulsating presence? Ruth's whole life centred around Anton — he was her little world, her god, her moral code . . . he was, in fact, everything to her. She loved and trusted him above all things.'

'Do you think she ever knew the truth about Anton and me?' Rona asked in an odd little voice.

'Yes, I should think so. It must have broken her heart,' Jay said with compassion. 'Then, when he died, it broke her spirit. That girl, who was made for love and happiness, has my deepest sympathy.'

'Anton loved her, I suppose, or he wouldn't have married her?' Rona took a cigarette from the box on the dressing-table and lighted it with slightly shaking hands.

Jay shook his head. 'If a man loved a girl like Ruth, he wouldn't seek entertainment elsewhere, my dearest Rona. It's an enigma why he married her, but I'll be prepared to bet it wasn't love on his side.'

'Jay, please . . . you're making me feel — unclean, tainted. I hate myself because I betrayed her — with her husband! If any woman did that to me and I knew about it — I'd kill her with my own hands!' Her voice soared a little hysterically on the last words and Jay dropped her brush to take his wife into his arms, tenderly, gently, his eyes full of concern.

'Darling, don't worry — you know I'll never treat you in such a way. As for hating yourself, that's silly! You said yourself — it's in the past. Ruth doesn't hate you: I think that in her heart she has forgiven you — and pities you.'

'Pities me!' Rona's head came up proudly.

'Yes — and don't act like a startled horse, darling. You nearly gave me a short upper-cut under the chin.' He laughed tenderly. 'Yes, she pities you and so do I — because you have to live with your conscience for the rest of your life. Because now you really know what it is to love a man as Ruth loved Anton — and I don't think I'm being conceited — you despise yourself for being so cheap.'

She buried her face in his shoulder. 'It was cheap, wasn't it? I convinced myself that I loved him, but I knew in my heart that I didn't — I was his mistress because I wanted him as he wanted me. There was nothing more to our relationship but physical attraction. I knew he would never marry me — and I didn't really want to marry him, when I was honest with myself.'

Jay kissed her gently and with a great deal of love.

'I love you,' he murmured against her ear. 'That's the only thing you need concern yourself with now. I love you very dearly, and I always will. If you ever feel that sort of attraction for any other man, just remember that I love and trust you — as Ruth once loved and trusted Anton Radinov!'

She leaned back a little from the

circle of his arms and looked adoringly up into his face. He smiled down at her. 'Well?'

'I was just thinking how much I love you, Jay,' she replied softly. 'How wise and how wonderful you are! And how very happy we're going to be!'

He kissed her nose, and said seriously: 'Not always, Rona. Remember, there can be no sunshine without shadow. But if we love each other enough, we'll walk through the shadows together out into the sun.'

★ ★ ★

It was bitterly cold at Cuddlesmere during January and February, and Anton spent long hours helping Adam and Luke about the farm. Luke was still taciturn and moody, almost sullen, but he had accepted Anton's presence, and the latter hoped that one day they would be friends, although no relationship between two men could compare with the kinship Anton and

Adam felt for each other.

Nancy's son, Gareth, was a thriving and healthy baby, now almost five months old; he was a contented child, and universally loved. Anton often thought that the only times when Luke revealed warmth of emotion and signs of tenderness were those times when he played with his tiny son.

Nancy was happier than she had ever been, for now there was a greater understanding between husband and wife. Often, when she sat sewing, or stood ironing, her thoughts would turn to the night of Gareth's birth, and a little smile would hover about her lips.

It had been a cold night in early October. An early frost had rimed the window-panes and Nancy had lain wakeful, struggling with the pain that threatened to take possession of her body, but hesitant to waken Luke. Her clumsy body seemed to find no comfort or warmth in the big double bed, but she would not disturb Luke, as he slept by her side, his jet black curls falling over his forehead, an arm flung outside the blankets. Gently, she covered him over. The slight movement woke him and he turned towards her, still half asleep. At that moment a sharp agonizing pain pierced Nancy's body, bringing a sharp, involuntary cry to her lips.

Luke sat up suddenly. 'Are you all right?' he asked, anxiously, switching on the light beside the bed.

She nodded, but her lips were tremulous as she tried to smile at him.

'Such lies!' he said roughly, but his eyes were tender. He swung himself out of bed. 'Can I get you something, Nancy?'

'No, Luke.' She shook her head. 'You'll get cold — come back to bed.' She knew that nothing could be done yet — it would be some time before her baby was born and it was too early to call a doctor.

He sat on the bed beside her. 'Are you sure?'

'Yes, I'm sure, Luke. Come back to bed, my dear, you need your sleep.'

He smiled. 'Have you slept?'

'No,' she admitted.

'It's the baby?' he asked softly. She nodded. 'This time — ' he paused. Nancy knew what was in his mind.

She touched his cheek gently. 'This time — it will be all right, Luke. Don't worry. This time you will have the son you want.'

'It was my fault before,' he said in a low voice. 'But that was the first and last time I shall ever hit you, Nancy.'

'Hush, my dear. That's all so long ago — I'd forgotten,' she lied. She held out her arms to him with a shy smile, and he came close to her, resting his head against her breast, holding her as tightly as he could with regard to her bulkiness. She held him tenderly, knowing that this was one of the times when Luke needed the assurance of her love.

'I'm scared, Nancy,' she heard his muffled voice tense with anxiety. 'I'm scared something will go wrong and I shall lose you. When I was a little boy, I had so little of my own — and people took things away from me, things I wanted desperately. If they take you away, too, Nancy . . .' his voice trailed off.

'Luke, no one can take me from you. I'm your wife, and — I love you.' She said the words shyly, but longing to hear him declare his love for her.

'You know, Nancy, I love you,' he said passionately. 'Perhaps I haven't always shown it — maybe I've not been a good or kind husband — maybe I've wanted to own you instead of love you — but I've always loved you. Since you were a pretty child hanging around John and Adam because they gave you fruit and sweets and trinkets. I gave you nothing because I had nothing to give — I was the youngest son and my brothers led me to believe you would never look at me or think of me as a lover. Then you fell in love with me and wanted to marry me: wanted to hear me say I loved you in return. Well, I married you, but I would never tell you of my love. I was afraid to reach out for happiness in case it ran away from me . . . '

'Then — you've loved me all this time?' There was a joyousness in her voice and he raised his head to look at her.

A soft smile curved his lips. 'That makes you happy, eh?' She nodded. 'Good. I want you to be happy, Nancy — it's all I've ever wanted. You promise you'll never run away from me?'

'You are so afraid, my darling, aren't you?' she said tenderly. 'Luke, I love you more than life itself — you are my life — does one run away from life?'

A fresh pain made her catch her breath and instantly he rose to his feet.

He remembered what Adam had once told him: he knew that he could not help Nancy if she was in labour. He had no experience of women in that condition and even the farm creatures sensed his ignorance, turning from him to Adam's soothing, helping hands.

'I'll get Adam, shall I?'

She laughed, catching her breath slightly. 'I feel like Damson. Luke, I need Dr. Kershaw more than Adam.'

Nancy knew that though she loved Luke, she needed Adam more than her husband. Adam, who was so wonderful with his calving animals, whose kind and gentle hands had a way with them, whose voice was kind and soothing, reassuring in pain. But she also knew that it was important that Luke should have her need of him — so she said: 'But I need you more than I need anyone else, my darling. If you are with me I shall feel no pain.'

His face softened. 'That's like you, Nancy. I understand and appreciate it — but I will get Dr. Kershaw. Until he can get here, I'll ask Adam to sit with you.'

He leaned over her and kissed her mouth tenderly.

'Don't forget now — produce a

bonny, bouncing boy, or there'll be trouble!' She laughed into his eyes and, grinning, he turned and left her.

It was a hard winter, but Nancy had the warmth of Luke's love, which was expressed in so many ways since the birth of their son, and her happiness in Gareth himself.

14

Anton sat by the blazing log fire, pipe clenched in his teeth, the local newspaper untouched on the table beside him. He was tired after a hard day's work, too tired even to read, which was often the case. He watched the bright flames lick hungrily at the wooden logs, half-thoughtful, half-listening to the disjointed conversation around him.

It was early in March. Nancy sat in a low nursing chair, her son in her arms and Luke on the rug at her feet. Adam had gone in to Yalton earlier in the day: it was market day and he hoped to get a bull heifer. Anton had volunteered to accompany him, but Adam had refused, saying that he trusted Anton more than Luke with the animals in his absence.

Anton was fit and healthy and

contented. The life at Cuddlesmere suited him: his skin was ruddy and glowed with health; his body was brown and muscular and even a little weather-beaten. Hard work, such as he had never known before, had given him a hearty appetite. He was happy — happier than he had believed it possible to be, surrounded by these simple country people. He knew the pleasure of relaxing a tired body in cool, linen sheets and the sleep of a healthily weary man: he knew the keen appetite sharpened by work and the enjoyment of good, home-cooked food: he knew the quiet talk of tired countrymen and hastened to learn all he could of the things they could teach him, these men who were the salt of the earth, whose whole life was wrapped up in the land they farmed. Yet Adam and Luke were not dullards: they could discuss a variety of subjects with knowledge and enthusiasm.

Luke and Nancy were talking in low tones of her coming birthday, which fell on the same day as Gareth was five months old. Nancy was almost twenty-one, and Luke felt that somehow the day should be celebrated in a proper manner, but Nancy, contented with her life as it was, was against any unnecessary fuss.

Luke glanced at his wife and smiled, a tender expression on his usually haughty face, and Anton observed the pair without being conscious that he was watching them. Nancy raised a hand to stroke back a lock of Luke's jet black hair. Her fingers caressed his cheek lightly and he put up his hand to take her fingers in his and draw them to his lips. Anton saw the sudden swift dart of joy in her eyes and looked away, conscious of intruding upon her emotions. He felt that he had no right to be in the room with husband and wife, whose mutual love seemed suddenly to radiate the whole atmosphere.

He rose to his feet.

'I think I'll go to my room and do

some work,' he said, yawning a little. 'I guess Adam isn't hurrying back from Yalton — probably he's having a really interesting conversation on cows with a few diehards.'

They all knew that Anton was writing a book. For the first time he was concentrating on a really serious subject, trying to project his own soul, his own experience of life into a fictitious character. He had been working on it for three months now, when the inspiration gripped him: he could not write to order. He had written about a third of the book and found that it flowed easily when he was really in the mood: he was beginning to be really satisfied, as much as one can be with one's own work, with what he had written.

'How's it coming, Anton?' Luke asked with interest.

Anton shrugged. 'So-so. I'm not yet at the stage when I shall be glad when it's finished — I'm still enjoying the writing of it very much.'

'Are you really in the mood for writing to-night?' Nancy smiled at him with understanding in her eyes. 'I know Luke and I aren't very interesting company for you, but please don't go away on our account. I'll make a nice cup of tea, put Gareth to bed, and we'll have a quiet talk. What do you say?'

Anton hesitated. Nancy was right. He did not want to write and her suggestion was very appealing.

'Do stay, Anton,' she persuaded him. 'I can see you're tired . . . '

At that moment the latch of the door was lifted, the door swung open and Adam came in, huge duffle coat wrapped warmly about his big body.

'It's cold,' he said, closing the door quickly behind him. 'I shall be glad to see the spring this year. It's a long, hard winter.'

'Come by the fire, Adam. I was just going to put Gareth into bed and make tea. That will warm you up.' Nancy got to her feet.

Adam crossed to the fireplace and

350

touched the baby's cheek with one cold forefinger, tenderly.

'Tea would be welcome indeed, Nancy. Thanks. Good-night, young shaver.' He peeled off his duffle coat, flung it on to a chair and held his hands out to the blazing logs. 'That's better.'

'You're late, Adam.' Anton had instantly changed his plans at sight of his friend and resumed his seat by the fire.

'Yes. Been talking.'

'Did you get the heifer?' Luke asked him.

Adam shook his head. 'No. Bad breeding — wild strain in him. I wasn't going to risk spoiling the blood in my cattle. I'm in no real hurry to get this young bull: but it doesn't hurt to look around the markets when I get the chance.' He turned to Anton. 'Animals all right?'

'Of course. You've only been off the farm for a matter of hours — what could go wrong in that short time?'

'There's no telling. By the way, Anton, I want to have a talk with you.' His voice was suddenly serious and Anton raised an enquiring eyebrow.

'Go ahead!'

'Not right now.'

'Do you want me to go?' Luke asked, suddenly sensitive to the changed atmosphere. Adam paused, looking at his brother for a long moment. Then he nodded.

'Would you mind, Luke? I might as well say what I have to say while it's fresh in my thoughts.'

Luke grinned. 'I'll go and talk to Nancy while she attends to the baby.' He went out of the room, whistling.

Anton struck a match and relit his pipe. Then he smiled at Adam. 'You seem very ominous. Tell me the worst.'

Adam sat down on a comfortable chair and pulled it closer to the fire. He paused, fingering his lip thoughtfully, before he finally spoke.

'I'm going to be very interfering in your affairs for the next few minutes,

Anton. Perhaps I haven't any right to be, but knowing what I do — I haven't any choice.' Anton's face sobered and he laid aside his pipe, leaning forward intently.

'Go on.'

'You're Anton Radinov, aren't you?' Adam asked quickly.

'Yes.' Anton nodded. 'How do you know? John?'

'John? No. I suppose he would know the truth. Actually, I would probably never have known your real identity — always believed you to be Anton Marshall — if I hadn't been talking to-night to an old friend of mine in Yalton. He's a great theatre-goer and a keen reader . . . '

'But he's never seen me, has he?' Anton said quickly, then subsided at a look from Adam. 'Sorry, I didn't mean to interrupt you.'

'He was telling me of a series of articles in a monthly magazine which gives the life-stories of contemporary actors and actresses — he was telling me how many of these famous people, who would seem to have so much, so often have a tragedy in their life. He went on to ask me if I'd read about this month's subject — Anton Radinov, a brilliant actor, still young, famous and well-loved, a genius in his own plane, who had been reported as dead after a fever epidemic in Spain only nine months or so ago. My friend, Jack Stonely, happened to have his copy of the magazine on him and he showed it to me. They have some remarkable photographs of you, Anton, really very good likenesses. I knew I couldn't be mistaken.' He stopped, waiting for Anton to speak.

'You're not mistaken,' Anton said slowly. 'Yes, I'm Anton Radinov — very much alive. I'm glad you know the truth, Adam. I've hated deceiving you all these months. I guess I might as well tell you the rest of the ugly story now.' And briefly he went over the facts, explained to Adam his reasons for presuming his own death, reasons which seen now in the brighter light of sane thought seemed poor and cowardly. Watching the change of expression in Adam's face during the recital, Anton realized at last the depth of his folly and how his actions must appear to a man like Adam Newman, whose whole life was run on straight, clean and consistent lines. 'Don't think I'm proud of myself,' he finished. 'I'm not. But what could I do? I loved Ruth too much to have our marriage dragged through a divorce court. I wanted to save her from any hurt, but she wanted her freedom and, I suppose, happiness with someone else.'

'Perhaps she didn't want to be free,' Adam said quietly. 'She certainly hasn't made use of her freedom . . .'

'You know something about Ruth?' Anton asked eagerly, swiftly, his hunger for her apparent in his eyes and voice. 'How is she?'

'She hasn't married again. She's been too busy having your child!'

Anton stared at him. 'What?'

Adam rose to stand in front of the fireplace, hands behind his back, legs astride on the rug, a typically male attitude.

'I thought you didn't know, Anton. You may have been a reckless fool, but you're not that much of a knave. Your wife had a child in December . . . '

Anton buried his face in his hands with a slight groan.

'My poor Ruth! And I left her to face that alone.' A sudden thought struck him. 'She would have known about her child before I left for Spain — why didn't she tell me? It would have made all the difference.'

'Why didn't you tell her that you loved her — before you left for Spain?'

Anton looked up. 'I thought she wouldn't be interested — that she wanted to be free.'

'That's the answer to your question, too. From what little you've told me of your wife, I guess she would put your happiness first. I think you've been a pair of fools — but it isn't too late, Anton. There's nothing to stop you from going back to your wife and child.'

Anton shook his head. 'That would be useless. I told you — Ruth no longer loved me — she said she was sorry that she'd married me in the first place.'

'A pregnant woman says all sorts of foolish things — things she doesn't mean for one moment.'

There was a short silence.

'A pregnant woman!' Anton repeated quietly, almost to himself. 'Yes, that would explain a lot of things — but there's no excuse for the way I treated Ruth . . . '

'Your unfaithfulness? I think that Ruth would probably have the strength of mind to put that behind her, to forgive and forget, if she could be reunited with her husband.'

'Do you think so?' Anton sounded like an eager child.

Adam sighed, a little exasperated. 'You would think so yourself if you would approach the whole thing with an

357

adult outlook. You're a grown man and you act like a small child. Anyway, I've told you all I know, Anton. It's your life — you must decide what to do. In any case, I'm through interfering, and here comes Nancy with the tea, so we'd better change the subject.' He turned towards his sister-in-law. 'I'm ready for that, Nancy. Strong and hot, there's a good girl.'

Luke followed Nancy with a plate of cakes and biscuits.

'Serious discussion over? Is it safe to venture into the holy of holies?' He put the plate on the table. 'I peeked round the door at one time, but you were both so serious and intense, I decided to stay out of it.'

Adam laughed. 'It was a very involved conversation. You were better off where you were. Gareth asleep?' he asked Nancy. She nodded.

'Like a top. He's such a good baby . . . '

Anton was not conscious of the talk that flowed around him. He accepted a cup of tea from Nancy, but was unaware that he did so. Thoughtfully, he stirred the tea again and again, but it went cold, untouched by his lips.

With a quick look, Adam warned Luke and Nancy not to bother him, and they continued to talk idly between them.

Anton could only think of Ruth, his life, his love, and the child that had been born unknown to him. Knowing Ruth as he did, he could believe that Adam was right in saying that her pregnancy had inspired the bitter outburst, which meant that she had loved him from beginning to end with the same sweet intensity. His emotions were numb with shock; he could not think coherently. He was only aware that he had left Ruth at the time when she must have needed him more than at any other time: he had left his wife to shed bitter tears for him, not only at his loss, but also at the death she had no reason to doubt: he had left her to bear his child alone and without his reassuring presence to sustain her through the ordeal. Staring into the flames of the fire, he saw only Ruth's face, clear, compassionate, integral and loving, felt once again the gaze of her cool grey eyes, and longed ardently to feel the pressure of her lips under his.

He was suddenly filled with a hot emotion that startled him and he rose to his feet, almost dropping the cold cup of tea which Adam hastened to take from him. With a cursory word to his friends, he left the room and ran up the old oak stairs to his bedroom.

He paced the room in anguish, clenching and unclenching his strong hands by his sides, wondering how best to undo the wrong he had done to his wife.

'Oh, Ruth!' he said aloud, gently. 'How I loved you — and still do! What am I going to do?'

For the last few months he had been reconciled to Ruth's loss, had been almost devoid of emotion where she was concerned. Now his love for her, scalding and vital, flowed through his very veins and he was on fire to see her, to hear her speak, to hold her in his arms. He went to the window, leaned his forehead on the window-panes and his hands on the sill: though he looked out into the night he was not conscious of the dark sky, lit at irregular intervals by bright stars, nor of the lights of the village in the distance. He knew that he must go to Ruth, beg her forgiveness, hope for her love and humble himself before her for the wrongs he had done, the way he had treated her and the unhappiness he had brought her.

Now that a decision had been reached he was the old Anton, impatient to carry out his decision, eager to see results, and he began to make plans.

He would have to leave Cuddlesmere — but he meant to return, with Ruth if possible; his friends at The Haven were very dear to him. He would even miss Luke's haughty arrogance, he thought with a wry grin. He would make his way immediately to London, go first to Ruth and make his peace with her — the thought of seeing her once again made his veins tingle — and then seek out Mark, his lawyer, for advice on the legal aspect of his presumed death. Once he was reinstated as a living person he could take up the reins of his old life — he paused, no, not quite his old life. He would be a different man now that he had learnt a little from life's experiences. He wondered idly if he would go back to the theatre — or whether to concentrate on writing in the future, with Ruth and his child as his inspiration.

'I don't even know if it's a boy or girl,' he said to his reflection in the window-pane. 'I hope it's a son — I've always wanted a son, really, although children have never really been included in my plans before. A son of my own! He can't be very old — didn't Adam say it was born in December — younger than Gareth, even.' He talked to himself excitedly, then, conscious of the sound of his voice, he laughed a little. He tried to marshal his thoughts into some sort of order, but they kept wandering back to Ruth and her loveliness, her shining eyes, and the inner purity that had been the first thing to appeal to him.

That night, as he lay in bed on his back, eyes wide open in the darkness, he consciously prayed for the first time since he was a child, prayed for a second chance of happiness with Ruth and pledged his life to giving her that happiness.

★ ★ ★

Three days later, Anton stood at the door of Gregg Randall's flat, his finger on the bell. He was immaculate in a new suit, but he was nervous and excited. He had left Cuddlesmere the day before, conscious of Adam's approval at his actions, having told the truth to Luke and Nancy, and with their strict admonitions to bring his wife and baby back to The Haven in the shortest possible time ringing in his ears.

Gregg went to the door, still in his dressing-gown. Remnants of breakfast were on the table and the morning coffee was still hot.

He was whistling as he opened the door, a merry tune that died on his lips as he stared at Anton Radinov, the man everyone believed to be dead!

'My God!' he exclaimed. 'Anton!'

Anton grinned. 'Aren't you going to ask me in?'

'Of course.' Gregg grabbed his arm and pulled him through the door, then slammed it behind him and stood, lips pursed in a tuneless whistle, looking him over.

Anton returned his gaze steadily.

'What are you doing here?' Gregg asked at length. Recovering his composure, he strolled to the table. 'Coffee?' he asked nonchalantly.

Anton laughed outright. 'Same old Gregg! Nothing ever disturbs your equanimity! That's the reason why I came here before going to see Ruth. I knew *you* weren't likely to fall in a dead faint at my feet.' He sat on the edge of the table and added calmly: 'Yes, please, Gregg, I will have coffee.'

Gregg poured him a cup and added fresh coffee to his own cup, then opened a cigarette-case. Both men lighted cigarettes — the only sign of their mutual astonishment and nervousness was the way they inhaled deeply on their own cigarettes.

'So you aren't dead at all?' Gregg said obviously, and both men laughed.

'I've turned up like the proverbial bad penny,' Anton told him. 'How Ruth will take it, I don't know.'

'This will mean her salvation,' Gregg said slowly. He stubbed his cigarette with a quick, angry gesture. 'She's been like a dead woman since you died — sorry, I mean, since we heard you were dead. If it hadn't been for Simon, I think she wouldn't have had the will to live.'

'Simon?' Anton asked quickly. 'My son?'

Gregg nodded, looking at him sharply. 'So you know about him? Well, I think you had better tell me what happened to you — where you've been all this time — and what the hell this is all about!' He said the last in a humorous, half-angry tone of voice.

Ten minutes later he had heard the story.

He took a fresh cigarette and held it over the flame of the lighter that Anton held for him. Then he sighed.

'I guess you realize I had hopes myself where Ruth is concerned. Well, you are and always have been the only star in Ruth's sky — so they would probably only have remained hopes and nothing more.'

His own love for Ruth surging strongly through him, Anton could appreciate the other man's strong disappointment.

'I'm sorry, Gregg.'

Gregg shrugged. 'Don't give it a thought, old man. She's your wife and I guess you're entitled to her. Although I'm inclined to think you've forfeited any claim to her, you great jackass. What on earth got into you? Why didn't you talk it over with me? Hadn't you always discussed your plans with me before? Why did you suddenly get so proud, Anton? None of this need have happened if you hadn't shot off on your own . . . '

'Don't preach at me, Gregg,' Anton interrupted him, laughing. 'I'm not listening to a word. I've paid for my mistakes — ' he sobered. 'Unfortunately, so has Ruth, but I mean to make it up to her, if only she'll give me the chance.'

Gregg turned away towards his bedroom. 'She will.' He went to dress, leaving Anton alone, but the two men carried on a desultory conversation through the open door.

Strangely, it had come as little or no surprise to Gregg to find Anton on his doorstep. It had seemed natural enough and Gregg merely thought wryly that in a way he had expected it to happen one day.

He was glad beyond measure that Anton was alive and well. They had been more than friends and he had mourned Anton: he was generous enough to be grateful that a kind Providence had given Ruth back her husband and her happiness, even if it deprived him of a happiness he had hoped for himself.

15

There was a silence in the room and Anton rose to help himself to a cigarette from the box that stood on the low table.

Ruth's eyes followed his every movement, as they had done since he first arrived at the flat, as though she could not believe in his existence.

Gregg had called her two days before to tell her the news: had spent some time with her later the same day to tell her as much of Anton's story as he thought wise, and to ask if she would meet Anton to talk things over. At first, stunned by Gregg's amazing news, then terribly hurt by the realization that Anton had been the one to deliberately hurt her, grieve her, instead of an unkind Fate, she had refused ever to meet her husband again. But with Gregg's gentle persuasion, his kindness and his pleas for Anton's case, Ruth had agreed to see him, but asked for a few days in which to think.

Anton had been forced to be patient, chafing at the delay. He had stayed at Gregg's flat since his arrival in London: in the days following his appearance on Gregg's doorstep he had contacted Mark Gantry, his friend and lawyer, and on his advice had presented the police authorities with a full confession. He had also seen his bank manager who, upon hearing the story, agreed to advance him a sum of money on a personal loan basis until his affairs could be straightened out. Anton had been surprised to learn that Ruth had refused to touch a penny of the money in his account which automatically had become hers on his death.

Some hours ago, Ruth had telephoned Gregg to say that she was now prepared to see Anton if he came to the flat later in the day.

It had been no easy decision for Ruth: she had experienced a great deal of pain and sorrow during the months following Anton's supposed death: the memory could not be put aside lightly. She had to consider Simon, too: did Anton welcome the fact that he was a father — was he likely to want Simon for himself in the event of the divorce? Ruth was under no illusions. She did not know why Anton had not remained legally dead, as it had suited him to be for so many months, but she assumed he had his reasons. It occurred to her to wonder if he had fallen in love and wished to remarry, but was afraid to chance a bigamous marriage in case the truth came to light. Had he picked up the threads of his old life only to obtain a divorce in order to marry again?

With the bitter truth that Anton had deliberately staged his own death still whirling in her mind, it never once occurred to Ruth to hope that Anton had come back to her, prepared to try again.

But she realized that she and Anton had to talk: they couldn't expect to use

Gregg as a go-between.

Gregg had offered to accompany Anton to the flat, in order to help him over the first difficult minutes, but Anton refused, appreciative nevertheless of his friend's innate kindness.

'You've done enough as it is, Gregg,' he told him. 'From now on, Ruth and I are on our own.'

'Well, I can only wish you both the best of luck.' Gregg went to the door of his flat with Anton. He laid a hand on Anton's arm. 'Just one word of advice, Anton. Treat her gently — she's a sensitive woman and she's been badly hurt.'

Anton nodded. 'I'll remember.'

But apart from the paleness, the darkness of her grey eyes shadowed faintly by pale violet rings, Ruth did not seem unduly sensitive when she opened the flat door in answer to Anton's imperative ring.

They exchanged glances, Anton a little anxiously, Ruth coolly. She was extremely self-possessed, showing no sign of her inward agitation. Anton realized how the past months had matured the girl he had married. She was a woman, beautiful but aloof, lacking the warmth he remembered so well.

'Come in, Anton.' Nothing more: no welcoming smile.

He had entered, looked around. Nothing seemed to be changed. Nothing, that is, except his wife and she was a stranger. In all the times he had visualized his return during the last few days, it had never once been like this.

'Everything looks the same.' The words had been inane.

She nodded. 'Won't you sit down?' He had done so: she had calmly seated herself opposite, picked up the cigarette-box and offered it to him. She seemed to be playing a part — the part of a hostess being polite to an unwelcome guest and rather bored by the process.

He accepted a cigarette gratefully. A table-lighter he had never seen before stood on the low table between them. He picked it up casually.

'New?'

'Yes. Gregg gave it to me.'

'I see.' He paused. 'You've seen a lot of Gregg since . . . ' he broke off, but she finished the sentence for him.

'Since you so conveniently died? Yes, Gregg has been very good to me.'

He ignored the last sentence. 'Was it convenient?'

'For me, you mean? Not particularly. Was it meant to be?'

'Yes — I was thinking of your plans!'

'What plans did I have?' She was patient with him: her role had changed to that of a kind person humouring an eccentric.

'Never mind. I'm a little confused.' He laughed: it was a dry, forced sound. 'It's all so — so different to what I expected.'

'What did you expect?' She raised an eyebrow in mild surprise.

He shrugged. He could have said: 'I thought you'd be glad to see me' or else: 'You — in my arms, as you used to be'. Both leaped eagerly to mind. But he shrugged and said: 'What does it matter? I said everything is the same. I was wrong. Everything has changed.'

'By that, I suppose you mean that I've changed?' She had no pity. She kept her voice light and remote: she kept her eyes from revealing that she still cared. She had taught herself to be proud, to keep her heart from pounding unnecessarily. It was agony to be with Anton like this, to talk to him as if he were a stranger, to be relentless and cold with him, when she longed to put her arms tenderly about him, press her cheek against his and let him know without words that he was home, that she loved him and that nothing had really changed, where she was concerned.

She steeled herself against her treacherous heart. She knew that he was unhappy with this unsatisfactory conversation, but she was determined not to help him.

He made no immediate reply to her question. He did not look at her: turned the cigarette between his fingers and studied it intently. At length, he looked up.

'You have. But that's understandable. So have I. Time changes so many things — even so short a time.'

So it had seemed a short time to him. Pain caught at her throat: the time without him had been eternity, a never-ending consciousness of loss.

'Why did you want to see me?' It was out: the words he must be waiting for. Now she must be careful: his answer would be sure to hurt, but she must not let him see her pain.

He ground his cigarette in the ash-tray. How casually she spoke the words. How easy she made an answer seem. But it was not easy. He could not say simply to this stranger: 'I love you. Can't we try again to make a success of our marriage?' Her very remoteness made it impossible.

'We've got to talk things over, Ruth.'

It was the first time he had used her name and he stumbled on the word and was angry with himself for showing his weakness.

'What do you suggest we talk about?' Then her coolness had made him angry.

'It should be obvious! What do you mean to do, for one thing? . . .'

She interrupted him icily. 'What *you* mean to do is surely more important? After all, aren't *you* running our lives?'

Her sarcasm pained him. 'It isn't like you to be bitter or cruel.'

'Cruel! You can say that to *me*!' His words had pierced her armour and for the first time he saw expression in her face.

'I'm sorry,' he said quickly, 'it was unforgivable of me.' Her face softened and eager to press his advantage he added: 'Sorry for everything, I mean, Ruth. We all have our mad moments and mine lasted too long, that's all.'

So he could dismiss it so casually. Her head came high and she snapped:

'I had my mad moment when I married you.'

He could not look at her. So there it was again: she had regretted their marriage — and this time she wasn't pregnant. So Adam had been wrong and he was wrong too, in thinking he could put things right simply because he loved Ruth.

The hurt showed in his face and Ruth felt a pang of remorse. He had tried to apologize and she had been ungracious. It was no use: she could not hurt him, deeply though she had suffered through his actions. He seemed so young and vulnerable at that moment.

'That was unfair — and also untrue. I'm sorry.'

He longed to sweep her into his arms, press his lips hard on hers, wipe away the memory of the long months without her. Something of his thoughts showed in his eyes and she stiffened, wary, afraid that her own longing would betray her.

There was a pause.

'Why did you come back? Why did you change your mind and come back?' Ruth asked him at length.

He spread his hands in a deprecatory gesture.

'I heard about your — our son,' he said quietly.

She nodded. 'You want to claim him.' It was a statement, not a question. 'I'm sorry — but he's mine, and no court would allow you to have him.'

He stared at her. 'Claim him? D'you think I'd take him from you? No, I wanted to see him — I wanted to see you, Ruth — I realized what a fool I'd been and how much I'd thrown away. I wanted to see my son, hold him in my arms; I wanted . . . ' he broke off, knowing he could not say to Ruth what had been in his heart.

She looked at him oddly. 'I had no idea that you would be so pleased about being a father. I thought you disliked children.'

He shook his head. 'I admit I hadn't planned a family, Ruth. I thought you were too young — maybe I didn't want to share you. Believe me, Ruth, it was not my intention to leave you, knowing you were pregnant. I had no idea.'

'I knew that, Anton,' she said gently. 'I never realized how much a child could mean to me, until Gareth was born.'

'Gareth?' She was puzzled.

He had explained briefly who Gareth was, described the family with whom he had lived during the past months. Ruth listened with interest, wondering at the expression in his eyes as he talked of the Newmans. When he came to an end the atmosphere in the room had noticeably changed.

'They sound charming,' Ruth told him.

'They're wonderful people — the salt of the earth. I'd like you to meet them. They told me to bring you and the boy down as soon as I possibly could . . .' he went on, forgetting for the moment the circumstances.

'You want to take me to Cornwall?'

The surprise in her voice brought him to his senses.

'That was the idea. I hoped . . . ' He could not go on.

'But I don't understand. You mean that you imagined I would be prepared to live with you again as though nothing had happened.' She rose to her feet, agitated. This was totally unexpected She fought against the wild surging of joy in her heart. He couldn't possibly mean it — she was mistaken, she had misunderstood his meaning.

Pride went overboard in that moment and she knew that if he asked her to forgive and forget. there would be no hesitation.

Anton had misunderstood her agitation. The mere thought of living again with him had obviously upset her. It had probably been furthest from her thoughts. So his dreams were short-lived. He would return to Cornwall alone, unhappy. He thought of Ruth as a wild bird, scared, flustered, woken from her quiet solitude by the clumsy step of a vandal.

'No, of course not.' He answered her question soothingly, but Ruth was in no state to notice the finer points of expression in his voice.

She had walked to the window.

★ ★ ★

There was silence in the room. Anton rose to help himself from the cigarette-box on the table. Both were afraid to speak, to betray themselves. The past half-hour had been tense, difficult, and nerves were very much on edge.

Anton stood by the fireplace, smoking, an attitude familiar to Ruth. How dear he was to her, she thought. The crispness of his black hair, the curve of his cheek, the firm, mobile lips, the fine lines of his slim body — all represented the only happiness she would ever find with anyone. How much she had missed him. It was wonderful that he was really alive, really with her — but for what a short time! He would go out of her life again for ever as soon as things had been straightened out and she knew what he wanted of her. The thought made her sad.

Unconscious that she had spoken, she said his name aloud.

The word rang out in the silence of the room, and hung there, in letters of burning flame it seemed to them both.

It took him by surprise — the longing, the love and the deep tenderness was so evident in her voice. He stepped towards her instinctively — and in that moment the cry of a child came from the bedroom.

Ruth tore her gaze away from her husband's eyes, rose and went into the bedroom. She returned with their son in her arms and went to Anton's side.

Without a word he took Simon from her arms and held the boy closely, tenderly, searching his face, wonder and happiness alight in his eyes. The child lay quiet in his father's arms, gurgling merrily. His tiny face wrinkled into a smile and his grey eyes, so remarkably like Ruth's, half closed.

'He's smiling,' Anton said.

'It's nothing but wind,' Ruth told him.

'I know.' Anton grinned. 'But smiling is a nicer word.' The presence of their son relieved the tension of the atmosphere. 'He's got your eyes, Ruth.'

'But your hair.'

'Is he a good baby? He looks contented.'

'He's both. And thriving, too. He makes really good progress every week.'

'He's quite heavy. *How* old is he?'

'Three months on March 24th. He was born on Christmas Eve.'

'That means two lots of presents from Mummy and Daddy at Christmas,' Anton said, grinning.

Ruth realized the import of his words before he did and watched the dawning realization in his eyes. She made no reply. Anton laid his son on the cushions of the settee, turned to Ruth and put his hands on her shoulders, gently, gazing into her sweet face.

'Ruth, I love you so much. I've always loved you. I was a fool — I thought you regretted having married me — I thought of an easy way to give you your freedom.' He drew a long breath. 'Easy! I've never done anything more difficult in my life than giving you up, Ruth. I know you once loved me, darling. Do you still? Do you, Ruth?'

She nodded, her heart too full for words.

He caught her into his arms, held her against his heavily pounding heart. Her face was against his shoulder, her body warm and pliant in his arms and the longing he had known for so long was at last satisfied.

Ruth clung to him and tears were in her eyes. Were they at last to know the happiness she had always longed for?

'I love you so,' she murmured against the cloth of his suit.

'You'll try again, then?' When she

nodded, he added: 'You're sure, Ruth. There won't be any regrets? It means so much to me.'

She touched his face with a gentle hand. 'Anton, I'm not used to you like this. You were always so sure of yourself. What happened?'

'I guess I missed my wife too much.' he said gently, and kissed her. In his kiss he said all that he could not put into words, and if she had doubted that he truly loved her, when he raised his head from the kiss there were no more doubts.

She lifted shining eyes with more than a hint of tears to his and said: 'Darling, when do we leave for Cornwall?'

THE END